# The Liars' League

Take three star-crossed Duncannons. Examine only their shiny surfaces, and it's easy to place them among fortune's favoured. Pierce the veneer, however, and not many would find them enviable. Consider:

Alec—once a legendary football player and now the CEO of a high-powered advertising agency. A workaholic, because his life has an emptiness at its core that demands distraction.

Ellie—his sister. Driving, ambitious. Today, the leading light of the local bench; tomorrow the Supreme Court. But she, too, has a secret emptiness.

Neil—the youngest, the least successful, but in many ways the most attractive Duncannon. Except that he once beat a man so savagely it landed him in prison.

The stage is set. Unexpected events begin to exert pressure, and what follows is an explosive chain reaction: first the lies, next the rage, and finally the murder.

And now here come the Horowitzes—Homicide Lieutenant Jacob and Private Investigator Helen—plunged by duty *and* friendship smack in the middle of their fastest-paced and most engrossing adventure to date.

As they struggle to discover what's meant by a liars' league they ride an emotional rollercoaster to a surprising and shocking end. And when they do find out, it's the hard way.

*by the same author*

DEAD FACES LAUGHING
DEATH OF A NYMPH
THE NICE MURDERERS
ONE MAN'S MURDER
SUDDEN DEATH

DAVID DELMAN

# The Liars' League

COLLINS, 8 GRAFTON STREET, LONDON W1

William Collins Sons & Co. Ltd
London · Glasgow · Sydney · Auckland
Toronto · Johannesburg

First published 1989


British Library Cataloguing in Publication Data

Delman, David
The liars' league.—(Crime Club)
I. Title
813'.54[F]

ISBN 0 00 232236 6

Photoset in Linotron Baskerville by
Rowland Phototypesetting Ltd
Bury St Edmunds, Suffolk
Printed in Great Britain by
William Collins Sons & Co. Ltd, Glasgow

For Elizabeth M. Walter—admiringly,
appreciatively, and, above all, affectionately.

One of the most striking differences between a cat and a lie is that a cat has only nine lives.

Mark Twain

# PROLOGUE

On the twentieth anniversary of his mother's murder, Neil Duncannon, roaring drunk, hit someone hard enough to go to jail for it. Eight months later he walked out of Atticus a changed man, a more careful man. In all operative senses of the word the experience had been sobering. He now distrusted booze, shied from violence and deplored the waste that had keynoted his life. He made promises to himself.

But as Mark Twain once said, 'Verily these things lie on the knees of the gods.'

# THE CAST ASSEMBLES

My sister was a distinguished judge in the Tri-Town Court of Common Pleas. My brother was a consensus All-American fullback whose name people still remember and who until very recently owned a mid-size advertising agency which, when he bought it in the early 'seventies, was a minuscule one. So you can see they were both achievers.

I'm the sibling who didn't.

If my brother Alec were reading this he'd have growled that it was my own damn fault.

My sister the judge was seldom as direct. Ellie's way was to ask rhetorical questions. 'How might it have affected tenure, Neil, if you hadn't called Dean Fisher a closet philistine?' 'Isn't it possible, Neil, that you might have made your marriage work if you had cut twenty-five per cent from your alcoholic intake?' And the topper: 'I wonder if a stay in prison is at all commensurate with serious academic ambition?'

If you're as discerning as I imagine you to be you probably spotted the connecting link among Ellie's rhetoricals: booze. It used to make big trouble for me.

The prison stay mentioned above was for eight months, down from twelve, and could have been much worse—Assault and Battery that fell an eyelash short of becoming Manslaughter. The pertinent bar room brawl, witnesses say, was provoked by me. I don't remember that but have no doubt it was so. Not remembering things is characteristic of the way I used to get drunk.

A year and a half ago, this was. Just the occasional brew since, so I guess I can more or less say I've kicked the habit. Also shucked off a wife, Karen having moved out of our house the day I moved into Atticus. Also, a career. When

I emerged from the slammer it was without the semblance of serious academic ambition, and so I stopped teaching and went to work for my brother. I became a copywriter at his agency. Not a very eager one, but nobody ever dared complain about that since Alec was two things in a highly noticeable way: protective and explosive.

Why am I telling you all this? Think of yourself as that psychological phenomenon known as A Stranger on the Train. In other words I *need* to tell it, and thus I've manufactured you. Actually, I've been ordered to tell it, get it all down in manuscript exactly as if it were a novel. Well, ordered probably overstates the case. It's been strongly suggested that tons of therapeutic benefits will accrue from the exercise. And I suppose I've become a believer, more or less. Having done so, I order *you* to sit there and read. Anyway, neither of us has much to lose that I can see. You don't really exist. And, unless and until I can come to terms with it all, neither do I in any serviceable sense.

The obvious time to begin is Friday, August 14, 1987, the day on which things changed irrevocably for the three Duncannons. And for a motley group of others as well.

The place to begin, I think, is in Ellie's outer office with me sitting there rancorous and resentful as usual. I hated that office. All that ice-cold maroon leather and expensive pile carpet made me feel exactly as I knew she liked me to, Lilliputian. So did the big, dark portraits on the facing walls: the Judges Lister, Burkhardt, and McLendon, Ellie's immediate predecessors in those hallowed chambers. I had been there twenty minutes. I had at least ten more to wait, I thought, thirty to forty-five constituting the obligatory heels-cooling period. I tried to kill the time by guessing whether Dolly, her secretary, wore a bra or not. Dolly was the type of large, healthy girl who aroused such speculation.

I perched on the corner of her desk. 'Yes, or no, Dolly?' I asked beguilingly. 'You can level with me.'

'My name's not Dolly,' she said, cornflower blues riveted on her word-processor, which happened to be changing its menu at that moment. 'And you know it's not.'

'I once had an aunt named Dolly,' I said. 'A favourite aunt.'

'You never had any such thing. You call me Dolly because of Dolly Parton. And I don't like it, jailbird.'

As you can see Dolly (Nadine Dambrowski) nursed negative feelings towards me, which is odd since I do not believe I am essentially dislikable. I have sandy hair, a nice smile, and the open honest expression you see a lot of in late-night movies—the ones in which innocence is thick enough to cut. I'm just a shade over twenty-eight, a good age for being liked, six-two and well proportioned. If someone told you I was a tennis pro you'd tend to believe it—I have that look. But I'm not. I stopped short.

My 'stopped short' list, incidentally, used to drive Alec to distraction. Tennis was on it (I really did have some potential). Teaching, yes.

The bottom right desk drawer in my den still shelters an act and a half of autobiographical drama.

I went to law school for a semester.

I played serious chess for six months (God alone knows what that was all about).

For one brief shining hour I owned shares in a cash cow of a fast-food franchise before losing them in a poker game.

And so on in the same abortive vein.

A pattern of defeat, smacking of Byronic self-delusion, was the way one of Ellie's shrinks put it a few years back. Causation rooted in family history. Well, it's not an outlandish view, heaven knows. There is a body of evidence.

For openers, consider my mom. What a mad, bad woman she was. Beautiful and angelic when drunk. Surly when sober—so surly, sober, that crazy as I was about her, I couldn't bear to be near her then. But when the booze was on her she was loving and full of marvellous stories about knights and fair damsels—her own, not Malory's—and though I was only eight when I heard her last I can still recite the chivalric order of precedence.

They called her Rosie the Rapier—remember? The fast-talking lady who back in the 'fifties sat at that table of fast, funny talkers and for a while was as famous as the rest of them. Going to be a great novelist was the contemporary consensus. All she had to do was buckle down and harness her mighty talent. Not easy though, if you hate staying sober.

Age eight, I noted above. In fact it was the day before my birthday. When first awakened by those resonating voices I thought they belonged to the party I'd been happily dreaming about. Not so. It was my mother screaming at my father. I got out of bed and ran to the window, getting there just in time to see him shoot her. He also shot the man she had planned to run off with. He only broke that one's collar bone, but he killed my mother. Then he killed himself.

The foregoing notwithstanding, it's still hard for me to think of my father as a violent man. He was so basically quiet. Around the house he moved in a perpetual shuffle, as if every bit of him, including his voice, wore sneakers. He was a doctor; a fine one, Ellie always said—dedicated, self-sacrificing, looked-up-to, until driven mad by that whore, his wife.

I guess Rose deserved her ill repute. The man she was planning to run off with would have been the third. And I guess my father *was* a regular Martin Arrowsmith—I mean, if Judge Duncannon says so.

The silence he shuffled about in was absent-minded, or rather bemused, giving the impression that important intellectual action was happening in his upper storeys—none of which had much to do with the life and times of an eight-year-old kid. But *he* had a nice smile, too, and brown eyes that people who did newspaper and/or magazine articles about him were wont to describe as wonderfully kind. Did I like him? Never saw him enough to know. Neither did Alec, for that matter. He was seldom home. Consultancy made a globe-trotter out of him, and between projects he showed a marked preference for the distaff Duncannons.

'A leading authority in matters of the heart.' That's a quote from a Barbara Walters look-alike, who then presented her television audience with, 'Dr Gordon Duncannon, cardiologist to presidents and kings.'

'If he knew so much about the damn heart,' Alec said once, 'how come he needed two bullets to take her out.'

But that was my brother in a rare moment of captiousness.

In this connection it's worth mentioning that a week after my father wiped out our older generation Alec ran away from home. For a while he kept doing that. I think the Nyes, our guardians (Rose's sister), were on the point of packing him off to New Zealand when midway through high school he suddenly settled down. The next thing you knew he was Cannon Duncannon—punishing would-be tacklers. And getting more than his share of A's. And never looking back.

End of digression for now.

I returned to the leather sofa and was about to drop into its cold embrace when Ellie appeared in her doorway. I looked at my watch. Curious, a good six minutes off the previous world record. The other curious thing was that she almost never summoned me in just that way. Customarily, the summons was issued through Dolly, as if some kind of strainer were necessary. I won't say I was prescient enough to sense a deluge from just two water drops, but my subconscious did store up the material.

I followed her. She walked with the innate clumsiness of the natural non-athlete. It was our father's gait, except that where he had been noiseless, she was a confirmed clatterer. She reached the chair behind her desk and dropped into it heavily. Not that she was large, mind you; far from it, it was just that she could never do anything lightly, even sit.

I've probably given you the wrong impression of Ellie, physically at least. I mean, I know it's going to come as a surprise to you that most people thought of her as an attractive woman. Skin delicately pale, hair dramatically white since her early twenties, snapping blue eyes. Most people were drawn to all that. Her figure was in stark contrast to Dolly's, but in a world of decidedly catholic tastes skinny has its votaries, too.

Cool and elegant was conventional wisdom's favourite phrase for her. In a limited fashion I suppose it applied. Limited in the sense that if you grew up in the same house with her you could vividly recall the times her temper erupted. Ask Aunt Pamela Nye about the bathroom mirror Ellie shattered, slinging a jar of cold cream at it. Ask Uncle Robert, her husband, about the fate of a certain white dinner jacket. And Alec could have cited his savaged stamp collection. As for me . . . but why go on.

She had just dropped heavily on to one of her cloned leather chairs when we left her three paragraphs back. I checked her out—the eyes in particular. Once I had been convinced it was in her power to enlarge the irises at will, for the sake of intimidation. A subdued rather than a truly snapping blue was in evidence today, I decided. That didn't mean the interview would be pleasant—they never were—but I was reasonably sure now it wasn't going to be brutal.

The phone rang.

'Judge Duncannon,' I heard her say and rubbed my hand across the grin that rose unbidden. (God, how she loved that title.) To further camouflage unseemly levity, I lifted myself from my chair and shifted over to stand before the full-length portrait of my father that dominated the far wall. I was fascinated by that portrait. He looked like a happy man in it, which, when you think about it, is an indication of art's possibilities.

Phone conversation ended, she called my name in that

aristocratic monotone of hers, clipped and low, as if sound above a certain decibel level was iniquitous. I redeposited myself in the chair.

After the moment she always devoted to thorough examination she said, grudgingly, 'You look fit. I haven't seen you in six weeks, and I thought it was because you had fallen off the wagon and were hiding from me. But I was wrong. I'm impressed.'

'Thanks.'

'Tennis?'

'Some.'

'And still no booze obviously, or it would show. I didn't think you could do it, you know.'

I began the tuneless humming—learned from Alec—that usually set her teeth on edge and got her down to business.

She went to her desk, opened the centre drawer, withdrew an envelope from it, and handed me a letter from my former wife. I had no trouble recognizing the handwriting—curlicues held to a minimum, all the straight lines sternly erect.

'What does she want?' I asked.

'Read it.'

'It's not addressed to me.'

'Neil, have I ever told you about your sense of proportion? It's regressive. You see things like a child.'

'You've told me. More than once. Many more times than once. It leads to how I'm basically immature. Which is either the consequence of the forerunner of my never being willing to accept responsibility.'

She didn't get sore. And that was the clincher to my growing conviction that this was an oddball day.

'Read the letter,' she said. And when I still hesitated, she added, 'Please. I've not had a pleasant morning. I'm tired, and I'd rather not fence with you.'

She did look tired, not herself. But I was a veteran in the Duncannon wars, and though I almost never won I did know enough by now not to fall into obvious traps. Buckle up, young sir, I warned myself.

But I read the letter.

Dear Ellie:

When I call, Neil hangs up.

When I write, he returns the letters unopened.

It's infuriating because there are still unsettled matters between us. You're the only one I know who can make him behave sensibly. After all, there's quite a bit of money involved, and I know how you feel about waste. Please help.

Sincerely,
Karen.

I handed it back to her without comment.

'What unsettled matters?' she asked.

'She wants me to sell the house.'

'Why don't you?'

'Because I like living there.'

She looked at me. 'I don't believe you. My guess is you want to spite her.'

I kept silent.

'*Sell* the house,' she said. 'Why not? Fair's fair. The truth is she's no more to blame for the fiasco of your marriage than you. Within her limits—her narrow limits if you will—she did her best with you, you know.'

'Doesn't everybody?' I stood up. 'Anything else?'

'Of course there is,' she said.

'Sit.'

I did.

'Out of the frying-pan into the fire,' she said when she had me where she wanted me. 'So foolish. So . . . *you*, Neil. The idea that you might wait a bit, the idea that with maturity might come . . .' She broke off, leaving me nowhere near a worthwhile grasp of the subject at hand. I stared at her. In return she gave me her adults-dealing-with-children look. To evade this I went once more to study art. My father glanced down at me unseeingly. Art imitates life.

Ellie sighed.

'I do care for you, Neil,' Ellie said. 'Whether you believe that or not, it's true. And I care for the family, and what it stands for in this state.'

I almost bit my tongue in half holding back the first answer to spring there, settling for the more tactical, 'I don't know what you're talking about.'

'Of course you don't. You have next to no sense of family pride. Tradition . . . status . . . to you they've always been empty terms.'

I called on one of Alec's best bits, his tuneless version of *The Battle Hymn of the Republic.*

'Doesn't it mean anything to you at all that a Duncannon was our twenty-fourth governor? At least Karen's people—'

It was then I got a glimmering. You, however, will have to wait awhile for explication. Sufficient to say here it caused my hands to itch for her skinny shoulders so that I might shake hell out of her. While the itch was still on me the door burst open.

The man framed in it was tall and distinguished-looking. He was also unquestionably annoyed: face flushed, hair dishevelled. The hair in question, incidentally, was as white as Ellie's and as straight and fine.

Irritated though he clearly was, he recovered his poise quickly. I thought I caught a flicker of recognition in the glance he shot my way, and for that matter he seemed familiar to me, too—as if a slight nudge in the right direction might dislodge a name. He was about ten years older than I. His voice was East Coast cultured, a soupbone kind of voice, the kind always inventoried as a career asset.

'Sorry, Eleanore,' he said. 'Nadine's away from her desk,

and I didn't know you had company.' And at once swept into an exit remarkably smooth, considering that dots of pink still brightened his cheeks.

'Who *was* that masked man?' I asked when the door—gently now—had shut behind him.

She didn't seem to have heard me. She looked abstracted, uncertain—a look to which the lines in her face were unaccustomed. For an instant I saw Ellie Duncannon not as my ancient enemy but as the lonely old woman she might well be one day. It was disconcerting. But then the lines shifted, became Duncannonesque again, and her grin mocked me.

'You've a streak of sentimentality in you, Neil. Get rid of it. It's vulgar. And of course it's excess baggage.'

After which, as if the advice itself were excess baggage, she waved a dismissing hand. 'Your trust fund, Neil. The accountant called yesterday morning, and it seems there's a wrinkle.'

And so we set about discussing my wrinkled trust fund. This was a thing we did periodically, though 'discuss' was stretching, of course.

There were in fact three trust funds—identical, except for the stipulation that had allowed Ellie to come into hers at twenty-one. Thereafter, according to the master plan, she bossed the remaining funds until turn by turn the beneficiaries reached thirty-five. The Duncannon chronology stood like so: Ellie two years older than Alec, Alec seven years older than I, and finally (by a year) in full possession.

How thirty-five came to be magic in the kindly doctor's eyes, I couldn't tell you. I can tell you, though, that he judged Ellie considerably more competent than either of his male children. Alec, it so happened, hadn't needed the money to achieve what he had—he'd always been able to raise capital elsewhere—but it was the judgement itself that stuck in his craw, and while it probably wasn't the *major* source of that big league sibling rivalry, it was hard to beat as a symbol.

The wrinkle smoothed, Ellie placed her hands palms down on her desk and studied them. It was as if they had changed character during the night and were now strangers. One of the pinky nails was broken. Ellie with a broken nail! I was almost shocked.

'There's something I want you to do for me,' she said finally. 'You're my brother and there's no one else I can ask.'

I reminded her she had *two* brothers.

She blushed and that, too, was remarkable. What she said, however, was anything but, since it described a condition that applied ten days out of every two weeks. 'Surely you know I'm not talking to Alec.'

'As it happens I didn't.'

'He thinks because he runs a modestly successful advertising agency the world sees him as Lee Iacocca. Alec is insufferable. Well, he's about to experience a come-uppance.'

'What kind of come-uppance?'

'An unexpected one.'

'Aren't they always?'

'This one will be more so.'

I waited to see if details were to be supplied. When it became evident they were not, I started for the door. 'No, thanks,' I said.

'Neil!'

I stopped. Old habits are hard to break.

'All I want you to do is deliver a package for me. Is that too much to ask?'

'What kind of package?'

She shook her head impatiently. 'Oh, for God's sake, does that matter? You are, after all, under some small obligation to me, are you not?'

'Yes. I never asked you for anything, but yes, I recognize

the obligation. And you know you can count on me for . . . a lot. The thing is, I won't be your errand boy any more.'

'How often—'

'Often,' I said.

She glared at me.

If she hadn't . . . that is, if she'd been a shade less the outraged *grande dame* contending with domestic insurrection I might have relented. But Ellie was always Ellie, and imperiousness was to her what spots are to leopards. If that weren't so I wouldn't be writing this now.

I left.

Wiley Tait was jaywalking across the street when I came out of the building. He'd been heading towards Ellie's. Seeing me, he retraced his steps, ignoring condemnation from a taxicab and a moving van, and waited until I came up to him.

Wiley and I dated back to pre-history, having met as kindergartners in Mrs Merrywell's Country Day School. Later we had been roommates: prep school and college. He was the first good friend I ever had. Rephrase: the first and only in the sense that I could say to him whatever I wanted, in whatever way I wanted to say it and be understood. And if necessary—it too often was—forgiven.

In common Wiley and I had lousy parents. His had been even more famous than mine. His had been actors. More than that, luminaries. Both of them. His father had been among that singular group—Bogart, Fonda, Stewart, Mitchum—who had only to walk on to a stage or a movie set to generate magic. Marvellous, in old films, to watch Jed Tait, drunk or sober. After the age of twenty-five, more often drunk.

Wanda Wiley Tait, the Soap Opera Queen, Wiley's mom, had once been described—by my mom, in fact—as the 'world's most beautiful banality'. On occasion she changed the alliterating word to bitch.

Wiley and I became *friends* a month after my old man

made an orphan out of me. This happened two months after *his* old man did the same to him by plunging the family Maserati, complete with Soap Opera Queen, three hundred feet into a Swiss mountain lake.

One day Wiley found me in the headmaster's basement, crying, stuffed into an inch and a half under the staircase. Big even then, he managed to fold himself in next to me. Not saying much, he sat with me for over four hours. After that, though our paths diverged often enough, we were never really out of touch.

On Ellie's thirty-sixth birthday—it coincided with a rare period of armistice—I took her to see Wiley as Romeo. Afterwards I brought her to his dressing-room.

Until then Ellie had never shown much interest in he-ing and she-ing. There'd been a beau or two, but nothing of any consequence. 'Under-sexed' had always been Alec's verdict. For some reason I'd remained unconvinced. I'd leaned to the view that the problem was Rosie. Ellie trampled on urges, I thought, because her 'whorish' mother was still stuck in her psyche, and Ellie was scared stiff she'd turn out like her.

Wiley changed all that. Ellie took one look at him in doublet and hose, and that released the tiger in her. It was some moment. I mean, I was there, sitting next to her and saw it all—the glazing of the eyes, the parting of the lips, the undersized chest beating in trip-hammer time. Alec had been dead wrong. Backstage that night the palpability of the thing made poor Wiley—eight years younger and not really prepared—blush a little.

Two years before this—with money earned from a TV series—Wiley had bought one of those old churches on Sunday Square just before it was scheduled for razing. He launched Theater on the Square, the culmination of a dream. The way some men were about money and others women, Wiley was about classical theatre. To him it was the only theatre. Dedication, commitment, talent, ingenuity, the occasional lowering of standards, plus a surprisingly good head for business in one so young—and he managed to keep the dream alive for longer than I had expected. On the night of that fateful Romeo, however, he was in hock to his ears, painfully close to having to pack it in.

Ellie saw opportunity and rose to it. She let it be known that her coffers could open to keep a theatre going *if*. Wiley interpreted the if correctly, and a bargain was struck. In so many words? No, Wiley told me shortly after, but clear-cut and mutually understood all the same. 'I sold what I had left to sell.' And though the smile accompanying this was not much of a smile, he'd added: 'I'd do it again, any time.'

They married a month later. For political and professional reasons (and, Alec insisted, sweet snobbery's sake as well) Ellie kept her own name. You could never call it a match made in heaven, but by and large they had treated each other with affection and respect. That's not the same as saying Wiley didn't live through intervals during which he was as plagued by her as Alec and I were. And there was now, I thought, as he grabbed my arm and hurried me towards the watering hole that adjoined Ellie's building, a hint of extra intensity about him, suggesting he might be living through another such.

'Where the hell have you been? I've been calling for a week. I hate it when you don't return calls,' he said.

He got Cokes for both of us. Above the bridge of his nose, marring his beauty, was a noticeable V of concern. He asked, needlessly, if I had just come from Ellie's.

'You guessed because suddenly I look older than my years,' I said.

His frown deepened. 'Ellie Duncannon is a remarkable woman,' he said. 'She's one of the last of the idealists.'

Well, hard as it was sometimes for me to think of her in those terms, the evidence was conclusive. Ellie Bluenose, I called her once, whereupon she slapped me hard across the mouth. Reformer, yes, but no pacifist, our Ellie. Still, whatever it was that needed fixing you could count on her for time or money, to say nothing of passion. But why was Wiley sanctifying her to me today? For reassurance? There was that feeling about it.

'A woman with strict moral standards, but fair,' Wiley said, pressing glass gently into mahogany, the way a barfly does when he's made a point beyond dispute. 'Though you seldom give her credit for it, Ellie's always fair. The trouble is, you don't understand her. You never have. I love you, Neil. You know I do, but understanding people is not your strong point. And it's not Alec's either.' He broke off sharply.

'What's wrong?' I asked.

'What I just said was bullshit,' he said. 'Sixes and sevens. Or eights and goddam nines. Whatever the hell that expression is, that's me today.'

I watched him down his Coke like medicine, after which he ordered us to change the subject so we made chit-chat for the next quarter hour or so. At his request I told him about the state of the art in the advertising business. Brightening, he told me about the production he was just getting ready to cast.

'The Big H, *Hamlet*. My third crack at it, and you won't believe who I've signed for the Melancholy Dane.' He mentioned a fine young actor with a reputation for 'serious' that rivalled his own. 'He's finishing a picture and dying for some real work. He contacted *me*, Neil.'

I saluted him appreciatively.

'Might do it modern, might not, haven't decided yet. Now, are you ready for this? I'm going to play Polonius. Play him fat and funny. Beards and spirit gum and padding on the gut . . . I'll have a blast. I was going to play the King, but then the more I thought about Polonius the more tickled I got. Maybe play him like a demure old Richard Nixon, if you can conceive such a thing.'

'I almost can,' I said.

'Want a bit?' he asked. 'Rosencrantz?'

I was startled. 'Me?'

'Why not? Who knows, the bug might bite again. Act Two of that famous play of yours might actually get itself written.'

'It is written. All right, half written. Anyway, you're crazy.'

'It would get you closer to Amy Ashbogen.'

I kept silent.

'Like her, don't you?'

I kept silent.

'So think about it,' he said, and then smiling—determinedly, I thought—he headed towards a rendezvous with his favourite idealist.

I did not return directly to the agency. Nobody who knows me would be at all surprised to hear that. On the other hand, I did not go to Pat Corr's and tell my troubles, which once I would have done. I went to Tri-Town Park, and there, on a bench, amid other enjoyers of summer's flora and fauna, considered the question of whether or not Ellie had a right to regard mc as ungrateful. In part she did, of course. Putting the case for Ellie would include sheltering, clothing, and feeding. Also educating. Also trust-sitting. Ellie Duncannon had done her duty, no question. But it was duty done so cheerlessly that I had grown up adequately fed, housed, clothed, and chilled to the bone. I decided it felt good being ungrateful to Ellie. I whistled my way back to the office.

A reception committee of two was waiting for me. One was Roger Henderson, the other that self-same Amy Ashbogen mentioned by Wiley. Henderson was the account supervisor on London Brothers Shoes. Amy—only part-time a person of the theatre—was his second-in-command. That is, she was the London Brothers account executive, reporting to Henderson. I was his writer. Despite the power of the Duncannon name around those premises—or perhaps because of it—he was not delighted to have me on board. Nor was I delighted to be there. Too bad for both of us. Brother Alec had so decreed.

Roger was a dapper devil, born knowing what to wear and how to accessorize it. He was a walking Sunday *Times* magazine ad: blazer, cravat, and lightweight flannels a symphony in colour coordination. In his early forties, he featured rich brown hair and a rich beige complexion, both artificially induced (or so the agency consensus had it). He had a brisk, authoritative manner, an enviable grasp of marketing buzz words, and not a brain in his head. No way, then, he could miss top management in the ad bizz.

Amy . . . well, now that was a different case entirely. I suppose not everyone hungered for her as savagely as I did. Too small and slight, certain carping critics insisted. And small she was—heels got her past five-two—but with all her femaleness artfully arranged. Moreover, her black, curly hair was thick and shiny with good health. Nor was she anywhere near as fragile as she seemed. Tough, Amy was—as tough as Brooklyn girls are meant to be. Just now, however, she was looking a shade rattled. Roger was looking as if he wanted me drawn and quartered.

Like Wiley, he too wanted to know where the hell I'd been. And then I remembered he'd scheduled a London meeting for 2.0 p.m. It was now three.

'Researching,' I said.

I described a sudden anxiety attack. Call it a crisis of nerves, I suggested. Was I really performing at copywriter's max? For instance, did I really know all I should about the consumer experience vis-à-vis our product category? No, I had decided. Hence a lunch-hour spent slogging from shoe department to shoe department observing, absorbing. Now, reassured, I could write the kind of persuasive copy a client had every right to expect, who plunked his dollar on the A. D. Duncannon barrel-head.

Poor Roger. He would have bet *his* dollar, his last, that I was moonshining, but he was short of the evidence he needed to call me on it. He was tempted to anyway and might have done so had I not borne a famous name. Instead he snarled something to Amy about rescheduling, and stamped out of my cubicle in a virtuous snit.

'Jerk,' Amy said when we were alone.

I should say here that Amy has a voice Pied Pipers would kill for. Husky, decibels deeper than was predictable from so slight a source, and mysteriously able to take unlovely words and render them lyrical.

'Him a jerk or me a jerk?' I asked.

'Crisis of nerves indeed. You have to give a shit before you have a crisis.'

'Good point.'

She glared at me. 'You cost me an hour, you and your phoney crisis during which I had to sit around trying to make small talk. Imagine trying to make small talk with Roger Henderson for damn near an hour.'

I gulped at the enormity of the task.

'Where were you really?'

'I met an old friend,' I said. 'You're going to play Ophelia.'

'You met Wiley.'

'I did.'

'Wiley told you that, about Ophelia?'

'No, I guessed.'

'He *wants* me to, but I haven't said yes. I said I'd think about it. The thing is, I detest Ophelia. She's a whey-face, a born victim. People keep offering her to me because I look like this elfin princess, but she bores me. I've done her three times now—Elizabethan, Victorian, and, could you believe, contemporary Italian. She bored me every time. Four scenes, two of them forty minutes apart. Everybody with attention span problems forgets I ever existed. Oh God, give me Ibsen. Give me Nora.'

I made sympathetic noises, which she correctly identified as mild teasing. But then, because she was still more than a little sore at me, she said, 'And when are you going to finish *your* play, Neil?'

'Soon,' I said and proceeded at once to the Duncannon Gambit. Developed through the years, this enables me to evade the interlocutor's gaze while simultaneously pulling wool over it. In short, I attacked. 'How come I didn't get a work order for the *Good Housekeeping* ad?'

'The hell you didn't. You got two. One for the black and white half-page, the other for the colour spread. Damn it, Neil, you lose more job jackets than any three copywriters.'

And so we wrangled a bit. And so my poor stunted play was ignominiously camouflaged by trivia.

She got up. 'How about eleven on Monday for the re-schedule?'

I consulted my empty calendar for no reason other than the pleasure of keeping her with me. For the dozenth time the thought that I might ask her to dinner leaped unbidden. As fruitless a leap as its predecessors. 'Eleven's fine,' I said, and she left.

Why a dozen fruitless leaps? Because I was terrified she might say no? No, sir. Because I was afraid she might say yes; afraid, if she did, she'd find me all shell and no substance as one or two had before her. And in her case I might not be able to survive it.

Her head reappeared in the doorway. 'Your brother's been looking for you,' she said.

'Amy . . .'

She stopped.

'I really am sorry I fouled you up.'

She came further into the room and stared at me for a moment without speaking. Then: 'Don't,' she said.

'Don't what?'

'Don't you dare try that stuff on me, Neil Duncannon.'

'What stuff?'

'I won't have you being sweet to me. I won't put up with it. I know damn well what you are.'

'What am I?'

'You're a runaway truck looking for something to hit, and I'm telling you here and now, Buster, it's not going to be me.'

She turned and departed again, skirts in a furious swirl around those slightly too slender but to me altogether delicious legs.

I went in search of my big brother Alec. He was not in his office, so I stretched out on his sofa. Tracking him down would not have been easy. While scarcely J. Walter Thompson, A. D. Duncannon, Inc. did have some heft as ad agencies went: two hundred employees on three floors of a prestigiously located high rise in mid Tri-Towns. This, in order to attend to $105 million in billings—up noticeably over the previous year and up robustly over the past five, a pattern of growth that earned it respect in dark, dingy advertising bars where the cognoscenti gathered, gossiped, and kept score. Whatever else he was, my brother was a considerable businessman, his sister notwithstanding.

*His* pictures were in sharp contrast to the judge's. Except for a minuscule family corner on her desk, Ellie's were of dark-robed, stern-faced magisterial figures. Alec's were mostly of his wife. On three-quarters of a wall—top to bottom—there was Margaret enshrined. You saw her swimming, skiing, sunning . . . Margaret as a dimpled child, a hoydenish adolescent, a student, a bride, always worth looking at. She was one of those blue-eyed strawberry blondes cameras made love to. And the only thing magisterial about *her* figure is it was exactly the kind that gets judged Best of Show in beauty contests.

On the sliver of wall not devoted to Margaret there was a mini-shrine idolizing me. You think I'm kidding? I'm not. My brother loved me. Yelled his head off at me regularly. Thought nothing of persecuting me hellishly whenever my shortcomings became too much for him—but loved me. I never doubted that. Never, never.

'Because you're cute,' he said to me the one time I asked why. 'You were always cute. No kid could have hugged a teddy-bear cuter.' You don't think that's much of an answer? Maybe it's not, but it's the only answer he was willing to part with. Maybe the only one he was equipped to give. And—perhaps because of that—I found it curiously satisfying.

Things like blood and love aside, Alec really believed there was something to me. Ellie didn't, and what a difference that made in terms of response.

I returned to the Margaret gallery. In a few of those photos she was accompanied by her sister Karen.

Karen? Karen indeed. On your toes there, reader. My brother and I married sisters. How that came about is not really germane here, but callowness lies at the heart of it. Callowness, fecklessness, juvenile dumbness.

Karen and I fell in love. Not with each other of course, but with the idea of how chic it would be to follow in the footsteps of our older siblings. And wouldn't we look adorable as a couple. And wouldn't everybody be just knocked out by the four golden Duncannons, dripping storybook charm from their cumulative pores. And variations on that noxious theme.

Karen was three years younger than Margaret, and though dark where Margaret was fair, unmistakably her sister. I stood studying them—one blow-up in particular, taken recently as arm in arm they dared an ocean with their toes. Both were in bikinis. Both clearly stunners, nature's open-handedness with them fetchingly on display. But it seemed to me that when you looked at Karen the liar in her stared back. Oh, not a mean liar, I suppose, just a chronic one. I guess the most accurate way to put it is that Karen lived in a state of mental inaccuracy, which made it vaguely exhilarating to lie and definitely fatiguing to be truthful.

And while I was thinking this the door opened, and there were the sisters in life.

'Amazing who you'll bump into on a lucky day,' Karen

said, aiming herself towards me. Her target was my mouth. I bobbed and weaved, so she kissed my cheek instead and then pretended that was all she'd wanted.

'How's Chuck?' I asked.

'Who's Chuck?'

Chuck was the yuppie stockbroker for whom she'd left hearth and home not so very long ago.

'Oh him.' She grinned and struck an attitude. 'Chucked.'

I crossed the room to Margaret and got bussed again. 'She's not herself today, Neil darling,' Margaret said, turning me so she could whisper. 'She really isn't. She's going through a difficult time.'

But it seemed to me Margaret had that wrong. Hers was the difficult patch, I thought, taken slightly aback. Deeper shadows under her eyes than I was accustomed to seeing, a sort of scrim of anxiety over her opulence.

'All right, out of here, ladies,' Alec said, coming up behind them. 'This is a place of business, believe it or not, and Neil and I've got stuff to talk about.'

'Talk to him about selling that precious house of his,' Karen said. 'That's what you ought to talk to him about. I gave him the best years of my life, and he boots me out without so much as a financial by your leave. It's not right, Alec. He owes me more than that, and you know it.'

I kept silent.

Neither of the others spoke either. What she had just said was patently absurd. In the first place she was something of an heiress, scrimping along on an annual income four times mine and larger than Alec's. In the second place 'boots me out' hardly covered the facts of the case.

And the odd thing about Karen was that at one point it would have been as absurd to her as to any of the rest of us. No longer. She had spoken. That reshaped the world—until she spoke again. Ever the slave of anything she said, our Karen.

Alec ushered the sisters to the door. Karen broke away

and pointed an accusing finger at me. 'You're seeing someone, aren't you? Don't lie to me. I can tell you are. Damn you, Neil.' She went out, slamming the door.

Margaret shook her head. 'Neil, do be patient,' she said. 'She means well. She really does, only . . .' Further explanation was beyond her. She kissed me again and followed her sister.

'Damn me if she doesn't,' Alec said. 'Mean well, that is. She'd go through fire for Margaret. Or for you, I think, with all her craziness.'

'What I want her to do for me,' I said, 'is stay a hundred miles away.'

'It would kill you to sell the goddam house?'

'It would kill me,' I said.

He glared as if this somehow made me ungrateful. Alec was the stuff great glarers are made of. Begin with size. My height, but with barn door shoulders and slightly elongated arms that gave him, on his mean days, a primordial quality. He had eyes exactly like Ellie's, steel-blue and easily lit for battle. Also a full black beard, fit counterpart for blazing eyes. 'Whole damn agency's been looking for you,' he said.

'Henderson's the whole damn agency?'

'A bigger piece of it than you are, more's the pity. Anyway, don't start in with me on Henderson. When clients love you as much as they love him, then talk to me about Henderson.'

Suddenly I felt tired. Over-exposure to my siblings' rivalry could have that effect. I dropped to the sofa again.

'Alec, fire me,' I said.

'Quit,' he said.

'I hate this business.'

'So you tell me.'

'You don't believe it?'

'If you hate it so much, leave. Walk out that door now and keep walking. What's the matter? You think I'll follow you?'

'Yes.'

He got up from behind his desk and strode to the window. He stood there staring out at anything but the street below, while I studied his back. It was a stupendous back, powerfully mascular. At Dartmouth he'd been a football legend. Cannon Duncannon—ferocious, full of the inner rage that makes for great players. Which he might have been except he had cement hands. That is, you could never throw a pass from further away than four feet and depend on him catching it. Cement hands do not an NFL fullback make—to Alec's everlasting regret.

He turned. 'The fact is I couldn't let you walk out of here because what would you walk into?'

'None of your damn beeswax.' A phrase from our boyhood, ridiculous and well-remembered. I hadn't meant to do that, but the words popped out and made us both smile.

He came over to join me. He put his arm around my shoulders. 'Go ahead, get out of here for awhile. Go play some tennis.' His eyes got that faraway look, the look that went with fantasies in which I was some sort of storybook kid brother, ever triumphant and yet ever dependant. 'God, how I used to love to watch you play,' he said. He held up his palms so they were almost touching. 'You and me, both of us, got that close to being great.' His face changed again, his Ellie look now 'Her fault. She wouldn't let you alone about it. Tennis wasn't important enough. It wasn't Save the Seals or the Whales or the Katydids or some goddam thing like that.'

'It wasn't anybody's fault,' I said, shifting away from him.

But that was pressing the hot button. 'Don't tell *me* that,' he said. 'She took your talent and nagged the shine off it. Kids you used to beat like . . . I could have killed her.'

'It wasn't anybody's fault but mine,' I said and started for the door.

'Remember you're coming to dinner tonight,' he shouted after me. 'Six o'clock. No later. Margaret's got to be at the theatre by eight. She's auditioning for Wiley.'

I stopped. 'The thing is—'

'Be there,' he snapped, shutting down the conversation and aborting any serious effort at wriggling free.

It wasn't that I didn't like Margaret. I honestly did. In addition to being a prototypical beauty, she was also sweet-tempered and generous. Give you the shirt off her back, let you look down her cleavage all you wanted. It was just that we experienced those long silences. I mean Alec, too. It seemed to me he couldn't think of a lot to say to her either. And yet I knew how desperately he adored her. On the night of his bachelor dinner the two of us outlasted the rest of the company, and, shedding the smoky shambles of the hotel dining-room, had walked down to the beach. We watched the ocean pound the daylights out of the rock formation at Tri-Town Point. We were very drunk, at that famous stage when unguarded truth gets spoken. And he said, 'I've got her, Neil. I didn't think I had a rat's ass of a chance, but there it is. Christ, if I lost her now . . .' Those gorilla shoulders of his shivered like a baby's.

As it turned out I didn't take the afternoon off. Nor did I get to Alec's that night. Things took a different course. 'A different course—' what a mild phrase for a chain of events that had the deadly effect this one did. And yet it began innocuously enough—since anything that happens at an advertising agency is innocuous, given a reasonable perspective.

Amy was waiting for me in my office with an emergency trade ad. It was for a small but treasured client, Cabot Office Supplies. (Treasured because Henderson, the Brain King's father-in-law, was its chairman of the board.)

'Not my account,' I reminded her when she told me what was up. 'Where's Rhineheart?'

Tommy Rhineheart, the writer assigned, was out of town

—on location for a TV commercial. She needed a pinch-hitter, she said. She needed someone she could give Henderson's notes to and know the problem would be brilliantly solved. Within the hour, she added.

'That brilliant someone is me?'

'Who else?'

I took the notes. I returned to my office to be brilliant. Ten minutes later I presented her with a piece of copy headlined: SECRET WEAPON. Subhead: 'Cabot introduces the ultimate paper shredder. Now you can buy maximum security for only $199.' She was delighted. Reminding me it was a trade and not a consumer ad, she suggested 'sell' for 'buy' and said, 'Give it here.'

In ten more minutes she dropped into the chair next to my desk with a grunt of satisfaction. 'Client thinks I'm a genius,' she said.

'How about the writer?'

'What writer? I haven't told her yet there are such things. Joke, joke. God knows what *I* would have done without the writer. And whatever that may have been, it probably would have taken all night.'

'But now you can make it to Wiley's and watch him audition Margaret for . . . what? Queen Gertrude?'

'Yes. Want to come?'

'Me?'

'Why not? Always fun to watch Wiley work. And for starters I'll buy you a brew at Pat's. Scratch that, a Coke. Unless there's something else you'd rather be doing.'

Deciding that even Alec might forgive me if he'd had a finger on my pulse just then, I allowed as how there wasn't. While she went back to her office to get coat and briefcase, I made a phone call. Though not to Alec, of course. To Margaret. She was understanding. In fact, I remember thinking she was bemused, more so than usual. I related this to the way she'd looked in Alec's office. I was even moved to ask if there was something troubling her and if I could help. She said no. I sometimes wonder now what she might have said if I'd been convincing.

Pat Corr's was dark and gloomy, the way good saloons are meant to be. Four-thirty and as yet sparsely populated. We found a booth. I went to the bar and ordered her beer and my Coke. As he fixed hese, Corr—tall, bald, with a long blue jaw, himself a sometime member of Wiley's company—informed me I hadn't been around. I acknowledged the truth of that and pleaded a severe case of near death from the wood alcohol content in his moonshine gin. He said that probably explained it.

Amy took a deep pull. 'I've always liked this place,' she said. And then without transition: 'What am I going to do about you?'

I sipped my Coke. I tried to keep my face expressionless, while hoping that the booming behind my ribcage was a booming in my ears only.

'Talk to me about something inconsequential,' she said.

'You once told me there's no such thing as a dumb good actor,' I said.

'There isn't. What's good acting? It's being vulnerable and in control simultaneously. Now those are complex things to bring together. Dumb bunnies can't do it.'

'Can Margaret do it?'

'What do you think?'

'She does a pretty little song and dance. And I've seen her throw a nice light comedy line. But Queen Gertrude . . .?'

She sighed. 'Well, in the first place Wiley can't afford to run a union shop, so his talent pool is limited. In the second place she's not nearly as dumb as you think she is. And in the third place she believes in Wiley. And if he casts her . . . *if* he does . . . he'll get a performance out of her.'

'Do I have to keep talking about inconsequential things?'

'No. You can get me another beer.'

When I returned she said, 'I got a raise today, and your big brother spent fifteen lovely minutes detailing my virtues.

Nice man, Alec. Did I ever tell you how much I owe him?'

'No. But I can see he doesn't scare hell out of you the way he does the rest of the world.'

'With certain notable exceptions.'

'Yes.'

'You, for instance.'

'The exception I had in mind was my sister.'

She nodded. 'That's where I met him, you know—at the party they threw for her after she was elected judge. It was a down period in my life, way down. It was . . . anyway, I saw this grizzly of a man, and there was something about him that made me think he was as unhappy as I was. So I crossed the room to him. All of a sudden he lighted up. He recognized me. He had just seen me the night before, as Ophelia in fact. He told me I was terrific.'

'I remember that party. Always wondered how come you were there. But it was like Cinderella. I turned away, turned back, and you were gone.'

She looked at me oddly. I took a flier. 'You noticed me?'

'Yes.'

'You never told me that.'

She kept silent.

'Why didn't you ever tell me that?'

'You made me nervous,' she said.

Before I could speak she put a hand over my mouth and kept it there a moment. Then she drew it back, but only an inch or so—held at ready, as it were. I shrugged acquiescently. She returned the hand to her lap.

'Anyway,' she said, 'I found myself telling him all about my itty-bitty ups and my way-downs, my ambitions, my anxieties, and he wound up offering me a job, a beautiful job for an actress. Puts money in her pocket and gives her enough flex time so she can make it to auditions, classes, and the like. My patron saint, your brother. When I have my theatre I'll name it after him.' Her expression darkened. 'Take that, Ashbogen mère and père.'

'Your family wasn't supportive?'

'In my family support is for math majors. Actors? Filth. In my family, they couldn't decide whether to ship me to Israel or go there themselves to hide in shame.'

She took another deep pull. I thought of the second time I had seen her, at a client-agency softball game two years ago, just after Alec had hired her, just before my divorce. In sweatshirt and cut-offs. Swigging a beer then, too (after a doomed but gallant effort to score from third on not much more than a pop) and laying the cold container against a flushed temple. Watching the pulse throb, wanting her with a sharpness inexplicable to me, a person of generally modest appetite. Our glances meeting, then bouncing away like frightened flies.

'You don't have to be Jewish to have a tough family history,' I said.

Her almost black eyes regarded me solemnly. 'If you're thinking we're kindred spirits, you're wrong. In my own way I'm as ambitious as any of my three computer-happy brothers. I *am* going to have a theatre some day. I'm going to be one hell of a hotshot artistic director and teacher. I'm going to be as pure as Wiley, except he can keep his bloody Shakespeare. I'm going to do Ibsen and Pinter and Brecht and a bunch of others you never heard of, and you're not going to stop me.'

'Me?'

'Yes, you,' she said. 'You should take that seriously because in case you didn't know it that's what's at issue here.' And then suddenly, as if some inner logjam had unexpectedly broken, she put down her glass. 'I'm on my way,' she said.

'I thought—'

'Cancelled,' she said.

Full steam, she headed for the door. She almost got there. Five, six feet from it she stopped, and now it was as if some field of force had become impenetrable. It seemed to me I could see her press against it. At length, she reversed, came all the way back. The drumming behind my ribcage had started up again.

'You weren't fooled at all,' she said. 'You knew I wasn't going to make it.'

But there she was dead wrong.

Hauling me to my feet, she said, 'Let's for God's sake go and get this over with.'

We did. Lying next to her, our hands clasped, I stared up at the ceiling and silently said our names. I reduced them to initials. Then, with my free hand, I carved these in the air and encased them in a heart.

She opened her eyes. 'What are you doing?'

When I didn't answer she shut them again. I began taking note of my surroundings: her bedroom. Through the open door I could see most of a small but attractive apartment. Except for the crazy-quilt pattern of our discarded clothing, it was neat. It was like her, I thought. Slenderly furnished, but elegant.

'A person could feel at home here,' I said.

'Don't you dare,' she said. and she wasn't smiling. She looked grim, in fact. And when she felt my eyes on her she turned towards me so that there might be nothing equivocal about the confrontation. 'I'm not at all sure this wasn't the worst mistake I've made since . . .'

She didn't finish. So I asked her to. Not that I was really interested in the time frame. It was just something to say while assorted happy fantasies collapsed in rose-coloured shards.

'It didn't feel much like a mistake,' I said.

'Bodies,' she said dismissively. 'All right, I'll grant you bodies.' She sat up, reaching for my head to bring it with her. This she nestled between pretty, breasts so that my nose, if it wanted to, could sniff away at the deliciously sweaty aroma of her skin. Or I could nibble at a nipple. I decided to save this for later. 'But bodies are *not* the issue here.'

'Still, let's stick with them a bit,' I said. 'And along those lines, when did my luck begin to change.'

'Luck? Luck has nothing to do with it. Don't be dumb.'

'Only two and a half hours ago I was a truck looking for someone to hit,' I pointed out. 'And you didn't want it to be you.'

She smiled, the kind of superior smile females reserve for invidious comparisons between the sexes. 'Words. Going through the motions. By then it was too late, of course.'

'By when wasn't it too late?'

'If we're still talking about bodies, probably around the time your sister called me.'

I pulled free so I could stare at her.

'Two weeks ago today,' she said. 'She called to warn me off. Though when you get right down to it, it may have been too late even then, bodies being what they are.'

Think back now ten, fifteen pages. Remember that glimmering I experienced in Ellie's office when she took on so about family pride and my deplorable lack of it? The glimmering I said I'd get around to interpreting? Well, we're there now. I had sensed then she was referring to Amy. No evidence, just antennæ. Just years of quivering alertness to sibling aggression. But how had Ellie guessed there was anything to refer to? At the time *I* would have set Amy's interest in me at snake's belly level. How come Ellie knew different? I asked the question aloud.

'My ex-husband told her.'

I understood every one of those words. Put them together, and they spelled Sanskrit. Vaguely, I'd been aware of an ex-husband, but since I'd never seen him around or heard much mention of him I'd found it comfortable to regard him as ectoplasmic, a wraithlike figment out of ancient history. Now I was confronted with an ex-husband on speaking terms with my sister. That gave him substance, but left me nowhere.

'Richard's my ex-husband,' she said, watching me. 'He wants me back. I told him no way. And then I told him about you.'

'About me?'

'Not *told* exactly. Actually, I found myself babbling about you, making claims for you, saying wildly overstated things about your character and so on. Anyway I guess that was my first clue there was more going on between us than met the eye. Between our bodies, that is.'

'Is Richard distinguished-looking and sort of . . .' I discarded the word that came first to mind and groped for another.

She suggested one. 'Willowy?'

'Close enough,' I said after a moment.

'Some day I may tell you all about the smart-ass he married—' she pointed to herself—'who thought she knew everything about everything, and beyond that wanted desperately to get back at her parents. But I'd rather not do it now. OK?'

'OK.'

'Except to say that I was very young and that Richard is . . . sexually complex, if you take my meaning.'

'Does Richard have a surname?'

'Grant. Judge Richard Grant. With an office down the hall from your sister's. Probably going to run for governor next year. You must know Richard. Everybody does.'

I nodded. 'I saw him today.' Face and form having clicked, a split second later the name made a connection, too. 'And I'm playing doubles against him tomorrow.'

A ringing telephone raised my eyes to half mast. I'd been dead asleep, and in those first seconds I had no idea where I was. The mound of Amy's hip clued me in. A glance at my watch told me that what felt like hours was actually less than one. It was 6.45.

The ringing seemed to gain stridency.

'Answer it, please,' Amy muttered.

I tried to say wouldn't that be indiscreet. The words formed clearly enough in my brain but were delivered as porridge.

'Have a heart,' Amy said, pulling the blanket over her head.

I lifted the phone and uttered more porridge.

'Neil . . .? It is you, isn't it?'

That went far to restore perspective. 'How the hell . . .?' I decided it was senseless to complete the thought.

Amy's head popped from under the blanket. She was alert now and interested.

'What do you want?'

'I've been looking for you everywhere,' Ellie said. And then, astonishingly, 'I need you.'

I asked her to repeat that. If she had, I would have held the phone to Amy's ear so that I might have a witness.

But she didn't. 'Neil, could you come over, please. I'm at my office.'

'Now?'

'Please,' she said. And then said it again. And then hung up.

Plaintiveness? From Ellie? I stared at the phone. And I think now that those brief moments served as foreshadowing, that in her own way, perhaps subconsciously, she had prepared me for upheaval.

Amy said, 'I'm guessing that was your sister and that she sounded troubled.'

'She sounded . . . out of her cage.'

I explained as best I could while I got my clothes on. When I was fully dressed I knelt by her bed and kissed her.

'Bloody blood relatives,' I said. 'Maybe I'll see you later at the theatre.'

She nodded, brushed my cheek affectionately with the back of her hand.

I got to the door and then returned, kneeling as before. 'Tell me something good to go out on.'

'Like what?'

'Improvise.'

The head disappeared under the blanket again. I nudged her, waited a moment, but when she didn't reappear, I got up and headed for the door again.

She beat me there—a dark-skinned nymph, heart-breakingly slim and smooth. She hugged me, then raced back to bed. I watched her sweet bare ass twinkle in the dimness of the room. It was hell to leave.

Twenty minutes later I opened the door to Ellie's office and shut it instantly. In practically the same motion I got half way down the corridor, moving like a crazed antelope. I was in the elevator before I really allowed myself to consider what I had seen.

An ass of a lighter colour: this one belonging to my sister.

Two blocks later, after crossing Jessup Street, I stopped and held fire. I shuffled my feet a moment, reluctant to acknowledge the nature of the roadblock, but then I gave in. There was no way, I admitted, that I could leave that scene without trying to find out who the other half was.

None of my business? Of course it wasn't. And I wish I could say now I was fuelled by fraternal protectiveness of some kind because even that, absurd as it certainly would have been, would outrank prurient curiosity. I retraced my steps in a hurry, double-timing the last half block, pushing to get there before he could leave the building.

And I just did.

Up five-three in the third set with the first two even, there I was serving for the match when suddenly I ran out of gas. No surprise. What with one thing and another I had had, to put it mildly, an active night and an insufficiency of sleep. And it was goddam hot.

Helen Horowitz, my partner, always a quick study, spotted my difficulty. She dropped to a knee, her shoelaces in spurious need of tying. She took as long about it as Jacob, her husband, would let her. Jacob, a quick study himself, said, 'They're stalling, Judge. Duncannon's about to keel.'

'Damn,' Helen said, 'broke.' And held up evidence. Ambling to the sideline bench, she sat down to study what might be done. I joined her there. The two on the other side of the net, having not much recourse, followed us—Jacob fuming.

Meticulously, Helen relaced her shoe. 'So stupid of me, Judge. I knew this morning it was on the brink, but I just didn't do anything about it. You know how that is. And now I'm causing such bother.'

'And delay,' Jacob said grimly.

'And delay,' Helen agreed, smiling apologetically.

Grant smiled, too. He had a splendid smile, a proper vote-getter's smile. Against his magazine-cover tan, it shone winningly. Yesterday I had seen him flurried, but now his sea-blue eyes seemed impervious to emotional storm. And for that matter, fatigue. The rest of him seemed fatigue-proof, too. He had one of those tall, skinny builds that heat and humidity strike out on. I hate that kind. That kind has a history of getting blind drunk on the eve of the quarter finals and then taking me out in straight sets.

'All's fair in love and war,' he said.

Guileless? Hard to tell. Judge Grant, I had learned, could speak fifty words of absolutely basic English and leave you panting for a UN translator. In this case it was harder to tell than usual, since he was looking at Helen, not me.

'Let's play tennis,' I said, springing up from the bench.

'Why not?' Helen said, taking my hand.

Jauntily, we returned to the court. They followed—a spate of unflattering comment about his wife's Apache heritage issuing from Jacob, *sub rosa*.

The set resumed. I aced Jacob, who instantly called, 'Fault!' but couldn't make it stick.

'Fifteen-love,' Helen said, staring him down.

Grant, in his prime a state-ranked clay court player, did stave off the inevitable with a pretty cross-court return I could have reached only in my own prime. But Big Mo was on our side.

Three minutes later Helen clobbered Jacob's sitter, closing out the match.

To the clubhouse for refreshment. And for Helen and me to receive the spoils to which victors are entitled—in this case the coveted Horowitz Cup.

The Horowitz Cup was a shabby urn rescued from the evidence room at Tri-Town Central Police Headquarters. It had an ear missing, a circumference full of defacing gashes, and was now four years old as a symbol. As an artefact it was considerably older, though not so old as to have attained with age a single shred of dignity. Seen detachedly, it was a graceless, ill-made, copperish nonentity, but we of course did not see it that way. Helen and I had won the Cup three years running. Twice Jacob, partnered by all-stars of his choice, had been thrashed to the point of humiliation. Buoyed this year by Grant's credentials, he had hoped for a better fate. And had earned at least a more respectable one.

'A break here and there,' Grant said sympathetically.

'And less questionable tactics,' Jacob said. He caressed the cup regretfully before filling it with champagne and passing it to his wife.

Helen sipped, then on to me. 'Jacob is not a good loser,' she said.

'Do you feel sorry for him?' I asked.

'No. Losing is good for his humility quotient.'

'Does everyone have a humility quotient?' Grant asked.

'Everyone should have.'

'Do you, my dear?'

'Hell, no,' Jacob said, answering for her. 'Apaches have them cut out at birth.'

'Good,' Grant said. 'Beautiful women must never be humble. It's against natural law. The very idea is a travesty. Have done with it.' Then, glancing at his watch, he got up and said, 'I have to be on my way.' He kissed Helen's hand, shook Jacob's and suddenly flashed his high-voltage grin at me. 'Life must be forgiven her little vagaries, has that occurred to you?' he asked.

'Now and then.'

He nodded. 'I was sure it had. One comes to recognize those to whom it would.'

Charm. He was good at it, the way you get only after years of commitment. Charm was *his* game. He played it with panache, with total self-confidence. He played it in your face, so to speak; big deal if you caught him at it. If and when you did, he'd grin, charmingly. When he grinned you felt facial muscles on fire to emulate.

But you also itched to take a poke at him, to see what effect a bloody nose might have on his CQ: Charm Quotient.

Jacob had been watching us. 'Didn't realize you two guys were so chummy,' he said.

'Hardly that,' Grant said, gathering up his equipment. 'In fact we met yesterday for the first time.' Back to me. 'Have I apologized for my bizarre behaviour, incidentally?'

'Yes,' I said.

Back to Jacob. 'I arrived in his presence as if savages were after me. Nor is that far from the case. It was a group of outraged politicians. I had forgotten a meeting, you see. And since that meeting was for the purpose of honouring . . . well, I'll spare you that.' Deprecatory smile. 'Be that as it may, I needed a substitute in my courtroom and could think of no fitter candidate than Judge Duncannon.' Back to me. 'You say I have apologized?'

'In substance.'

'Grey cells. In one's late thirties deterioration becomes a

problem.' Shifting now to Helen. 'Remain thirty-five, my dear, for the sake of your grey cells.'

'I'm forty-three,' she said.

'Incredible,' he said. And repeated the word to show one and all how deeply felt it was. 'Mrs Horowitz, you are an exceptional woman.' Then back to me a final time. 'What a pity it is for exceptional men when exceptional women turn out to have prior claims on them.'

Had a signal been sent? Was I being warned off (Amy, that is)? I couldn't say for certain. I couldn't even say, for certain, that I wasn't being invited to something. The judge was enjoying himself at my expense. That much I did feel certain of, taking me like his namesake took Richmond.

A bow to Helen born in some tony Main Line dancing school, and he was gone.

The silence he left behind was inexplicably downbeat, as if in some mysterious way all three of us had been siphoned out of vital quarts of life force. Shaking myself into speech, I asked Helen, 'Do you like him?' I asked that because there wasn't much doubt that he liked her. For upwards of two hours the alert blue eyes had missed nary a jounce or bounce of her. In fact, of the group, only Jacob had seemed unable to stir his honour's libido. I wondered if he'd noticed.

Helen shot me a warning glance. It said: Fool, get off this. Do I want my Jacob on a rampage?

'I scarcely know him,' she said in answer to my question. 'What's under all that smoothness, Jacob?'

'More smoothness,' he said. 'He reminds me of Croker. In *Dombey and Son*. Always smiling and showing his lethal white teeth. Downtown they call him the Happy Hanging Judge. In case you're wondering, that's why I asked him to be my partner.' He turned to me. 'What was all that about life's little vagaries?'

'Beats me. Just the way he talks, I guess.'

He studied me.

'Jacob, cut out being a cop,' Helen said. But then she said, 'Who's the other exceptional woman?'

'Who says there is one?'

'I do.'

'His former wife,' I said.

Jacob whistled. Fixing his stare on a henna-headed person —in electric blue blazer and sunburnt designer jeans—he caused a coffee spill, a coughing fit, and an abrupt departure, but I knew he wasn't thinking about any of that. He was thinking about me. 'How's Karen?' he asked suddenly.

'Why?'

'Just a simple question,' he said. 'Don't get defensive about it. She lived next door to me for three years, didn't she? Besides, Helen's interested.'

'Are you?' I asked.

'Not very.'

And then we both waited for Jacob who with abstracted gentleness kept tapping an index finger against a bicuspid. Finally he said, 'I know some women are worth considerably more than others, but is this a case in point?'

'Yes.'

'If you had to bet your life on it?'

'Come on, Jacob, spell it out.'

'His Honour is reputed to have Family friends.'

'What the hell does that mean?'

A waiter came by with word he was wanted on the phone, so he was saved from elaborating.

'Is he kidding?' I asked Helen when he was gone. 'All right, I'll buy it that Grant is something more than a powder-puff. But a world class menace?'

'Jacob wouldn't kid about a thing like that. He likes you too much. How deeply involved are you?'

So I told her, invoking a decent reticence here and there. She listened passionately in the way that she and very few others could. It brought back the night of Karen's defection —Helen sitting in front of her fireplace, her large dark eyes fixed on me, her large, big-knuckled hands quiet in her lap, her black lace shawl graceful over her shoulders, sharing whatever it was I was mourning (certainly not Karen). Around 4.0 a.m., moved by some inchoate need or erratic impulse, I made a pass. She kissed my lips, removed my hand from her breast and said, 'I'm Jacob's.' The fierce listening then resumed as if uninterrupted. Except for the smile trace, which lingered a moment like breath on glass.

The Horowitzes had been our first friends when Karen and I, as newlyweds, moved into the neighbourhood. They were cops: Jacob a homicide cop, Helen now an entrepreneurial cop—her PI business exactly a month old. Before that she'd been a Tri-Town juvenile cop.

But to describe Jacob as a cop and leave it at that would be to understate criminally. In our neck of the woods—the Tri-Towns was a bedroom community for New York City—he was a phenomenon. He was a tourist attraction, a conversation piece, a landmark of a sort. He even had a certain impact on real estate values. As in: 'Not only are the schools above average, Mrs Smith, but maybe you'll sleep a bit better knowing that the house with the green fence and mullioned windows belongs to Lieutenant Horowitz.' His cases got ink. He'd been on *Sixty Minutes* and *The Today Show*. And on loan, more than a few times, to the FBI and the NYPD. Three major publishers were reputedly interested in ghosting a book for him. In short, Lieutenant Jacob Horowitz was a brilliant police officer with a record gaudy enough to disenchant a significant number of those who controlled his destiny. Another way of putting it is that he'd been stuck in grade seven years now, at least three years longer than was decent.

Even I, self-absorbed as I usually am, had known some of this the morning I caught him stealing my newspaper. 'Buy you another, kid,' he called out, while sliding into an unmarked Chevvy with a police sergeant as driver. That night he was around to apologize. Paper boy had forgotten to deliver his. He'd tried to plant an item germane to a case and had urgently needed to know if he'd been successful. I took the purloined paper from him and told him that for a drink the Duncannons would be willing to keep their mouths shut. He grinned, invited us over, and that's how it started. When the four of us began to play tennis together, enjoyably, the friendship ripened. I had taught Jacob chess, at which he was a natural, having been blessed with the two necessary attributes—mental tenacity and a wild-assed imagination. He—and Helen, always, always Helen—had done what they could for me during my months as jailbird. And after Karen left, it was Jacob who created the Horowitz Cup, his way of underscoring whose side he was on.

Jacob was a large, lumbering man whose gait was a subterfuge. Slow-moving, he wanted to be construed as slow-thinking. It was a misconception he established more often than not, and he considered it his competitive edge.

Helen was generously made, too, and dark as an Apache, which one-eighth of her was. At forty-three, two years younger than her husband, she was probably more beautiful than she had been a decade earlier. The cheekbones—once merely striking—were now compelling. Also, there was an aura about her that made you think she'd lived three previous lives before arriving at this era's. Younger men were always falling in love with her. As already demonstrated, she was gentle but firm with us.

Jacob returned. Looking up, I saw him pause at the room's entrance and glance towards the tennis court for a moment. A curious glance. An element of nostalgia in it as if the court stood for a simpler, pleasanter time. The glance flicked towards me but gave nothing away. Having reached the table, he lifted the Horowitz Cup as if it were Aladdin's and he had a job for its genie to do. But then he put it down firmly. Now he focused on me in a way that shut out everything that wasn't the two of us: no noises, no other guests in the clubhouse, no Helen. Just the two of us in a vacuum of Jacob's making. I sucked in my breath.

'Bad news,' he said.

'What?'

'Maybe you better come with me. Down to the locker-room. Some place quiet.'

I shook my head.

He nodded. 'That call . . . It was Cox, my boss. He said your sister's been raped and murdered.'

# INTERMISSION

In its heyday Blessed Mary had been the most admired of the four churches that graced the Tri-Towns' Sunday Square. Arched vaults, Gothic tracery and stained-glass windows had delighted parishioners in this heyday, a hundred years ago. Heyday long past, it had been rescued in the nick of time from Demolition Day—by Wiley Tait. Now as his 'Theater in the Square' it had regained respect if not grandeur. And it was still beautiful, though with the beauty of an old woman to whom not much is left but bone structure. Moreover, particularly during autumn fogs or gloomy spring drenchings, it did sometimes look a bit put upon. You could construe its squarish proportions as a shade affronted, as if it worried that the Fates might be having it on. Was there a calculated slur here, a tasteless suggestion that Religion was no more than the flip side of Theater?

One step inside, however, and this churchy edginess became irrelevant. Inside, Wiley's belonged to its Players. Masks of Comedy and Tragedy, nailed-up bits of costume, yellowing photos, time-honoured programmes and posters covered almost every inch of its walls. These were panelled in rich, dark walnut. Not by any stretch a munificent theatre, it was clearly a comfortable theatre. Wiley Tait had been stage-struck from the time he could walk. His theatre was the expression of that, and no sensible woman could enter it and think she came first in his life.

# STAGE STRUCK . . .
# WITH A BLUNT INSTRUMENT

## CHAPTER 1

The moment Jacob opened the door to George Cox's office, he wished he hadn't. The mayor was there. Everybody in Tri-Town officialdom understood that Mayor Knudsen was unhappy these days, and since misery was not a condition regarding which the mayor was prepared to be stoical, it followed that the object of his visit was to produce an unhappy Captain Cox. Finding them paired this way would fail to bring out the best in Jacob, he knew. An ample body of experience indicated that if he were not careful he would end by saying or doing something Helen would later label damn foolishness. He also knew how elusive it was, that state of being careful.

Cox and Jacob had graduated together from the police academy—Jacob first in his class; Cox thirty-seventh out of one hundred and eighty. But Cox had turned out much the better career planner. He was a small, thin man with a bandbox smartness to him. He wore excellent blue pin-striped suits with blue or white button-down broadcloth shirts and blue or red regimental striped ties. His narrow black moustache was so precise it looked painted on. To Cox, 'headline murders' were anathema. He owed his success to mundane murders, to the highly efficient management of highly routine homicides. He relished police procedure, took reassurance from the probabilities implied: for *x* hours expended, results at a predictable level. Increase the hours, improve the quality of the results. He trusted that formula, saw it as a still point in a turning world. There was every reason for Cox and Jacob to be antipathetic to each other and only one to explain the mutual respect that actually existed: they were both unequivocally honest men.

Mayor Knudsen, too, hated headlines. Headlines were all well and good for a certain type of politician, an ambitious one. Knudsen and ambition had parted company years ago. Now, with Tri-Towns' mayoralty, he had reached as high a pinnacle as was comfortable for him and wanted merely to roost there. To that end a smidgin of publicity was useful, a smidgin—not the white-hot glare under which he'd been frying for the past several days.

Knudsen was stocky, fair, fiftyish. He owned a booming laugh and a convivial style. He owned these but kept them by and large in a bureau drawer, nestled among his showier socks and handkerchiefs, dressing himself in them only on meet-the-public mornings. On other mornings, Jacob thought, he would have looked at home in the prow of a Viking ship. He had the kind of face that went with horned helmets—thick, red lips, tiny blue nails for eyes, and the pillager's perpetual scowl.

As Jacob opened the door Knudsen growled at him. 'The Great Detective himself,' he said. 'Come in, come in, Lieutenant Horowitz. What an honour.'

''Morning, Mayor,' Jacob said. And to Cox: 'You wanted me?'

'Sit,' Cox said.

Jacob took the indicated chair. 'Nice out,' he said. This was greeted by a heavy silence, so he elaborated. 'My old grandfather used to say about days like this that they were gifts, doled out, so many to a customer.'

'Did he?' Knudsen leaned forward. 'And about murder investigations where well-known and respected parties get blown away, did your old grampa have anything wise to say about that?'

Jacob shrugged. 'He might have said Rome wasn't built in a day.'

Knudsen turned to Cox. 'A day? How long has it been, Captain?'

'Eight days.'

'That's correct,' Knudsen said. 'You know how he knows?' The newspaper which had been folded in his lap now became a Viking's club, and he whirled it in the air to scare Saxons. 'He read it here.'

'The *Courier* always gets a little over-excited,' Jacob said. 'But I don't see why we should.'

Knudsen unrolled the newspaper. He flattened it on the desk. As if they were daisy petals, he ripped away the pages that separated him from the editorial he wanted to quote. He stared at Jacob. In his irises Jacob could see tiny twin hammers readying for the tiny blue nails.

'"It's been said that a people gets the government it deserves. Certainly that seems to be true these days in the Tri-Towns. Judge Duncannon was brutally raped and murdered eight days ago. The kind of government we deserve has generated the kind of police department that has generated, as far as we can tell, not a single lead. Mayor Knudsen, is this why we elected you?'

'Goddam yellow journalists,' Cox said.

'Know what your trouble is, Horowitz?' Knudsen demanded.

Certain this was not a question he could answer profitably, Jacob kept silent. But self-restraint earned him little.

'I'll tell you what it is. Civil Service, that's your trouble. You don't have to get out there on the stump.' Back once more to Cox, forgetting apparently that Civil Service was a trouble common to captain and lieutenant alike. 'He thinks it's easy making speeches, kissing babies, doing favours . . . all the shit a politician's got to do to get the public behind him. He thinks—'

Jacob held up his hand. Perhaps it was the suddenness

of the gesture. Or the simple surprise of being interrupted, an experience rare for the mayor around Tri-Town Hall. At any rate he cut off abruptly.

'Public sentiment is everything,' Jacob said. 'With it, nothing can fail; against it, nothing can succeed. A. Lincoln.'

The silence that greeted this was at first only sullen. Outrage fed it, until at last Knudsen was on his feet, stalking to the door, his cheeks mantled in a deep Viking flush. At the door he stopped and seemed to vibrate for a moment.

'Cox, I'm warning you. You better kick his ass in gear. Not tomorrow, not the next day. Now!' Exit, door slamming.

Cox did his famous trick of building steeples with fingers. It had been learned in his police academy days as an aid to temper-keeping. Seconds passed. Jacob guessed the device was not going to have its desired effect.

'You goddam smart-ass. Why do you have to be a smart-ass all the time?'

'Not all the time. Just with him.'

'Not just with him. With the Commissioner, too. With anyone you think is not quite as bright as you are.'

'Commissioner McCracken loves me.'

'Commissioner McCracken's scared stiff of you.'

'Got a card from him just this morning. It said, "Bermuda's fine. Wish you were here."'

'Commissioner McCracken's not in Bermuda. He's in Jamaica.'

'Yes, but does he know that?'

'Very funny. You think everything's funny. You're even crazy enough to think Knudsen's funny. But you're wrong, and one of these days they're going to get you, Jacob.'

Jacob thought about that for a moment. Then he said, 'I know. Just like I know it probably would have happened already if it hadn't been for you.'

Taken slightly aback, Cox made noises in his throat. These, though unintelligible, were communicative, and Jacob grinned. 'So, by the way, thanks,' he said.

On Cox's desk was a souvenir bullet, a fifty-calibre slug with his Marine regiment number stencilled on it. He had carried it through two campaigns in Viet Nam and through three administrations in the Tri-Towns. He thought of it as magic, as a survival totem. But it had collateral applications as well. It was ideal for desk bashing—a variety of scars and gouges attested to that. It was also useful for mood changes. He could pick it up, roll it in his fingers long enough to stop a conversation. Or bridge a gap in one. Or effect a transition.

As in: 'How's Helen?'

'Still waiting for her first client,' Jacob said.

'And when she gets it, it'll be some joker wants his wife tailed. And her second case will be the same. And her third. Because that's the kind of world we live in. She'll grow cynical and hard, Jacob, and you'll rue each day you let her stay out there in the cold.'

'*Let?* You think she's changed that much in five weeks?'

'Anyway I miss her,' Cox said.

Jacob nodded.

'Damn it, next thing I'll be blubbing. Bring me up to speed on this Duncannon mess.'

Cox, Jacob knew, was already as up to speed as he wanted to be, so that the briefing was meant for Jacob's benefit rather than his own. It was a way of prodding Jacob towards synthesis, an aid in separating wheat from chaff. Typically 'up-to-speed' sessions were scheduled a week or so into a major case. Both men thoroughly understood the operative fiction, but 'up-to-speed' had been hallowed by years of working together, while the sessions sometimes took surprisingly useful turns.

'We know what we knew,' Jacob said. 'Death due to skull fracture.'

'Due to being struck with a blunt instrument,' Cox said.

'In a manner of speaking—the steel-plated lower corner of a desk.'

'Tell me about the piece,' Cox said.

'Fifteen feet from the corpse, under a chair, was an unfired, fully loaded .22 registered to her. All prints wiped clean. Time of death from around 8.0 to 10.0 p.m. Friday, August 14th, according to the Medical Examiner. Body found early Saturday morning by a cleaning woman. Where? In one of the two dressing-rooms attached to the "Second Space" at Wiley Tait's Theater in the Square. Ever been there? At Second Space, I mean.'

'I hate actors,' Cox said tangentially though vehemently.

'Brand new,' Jacob said. 'Only fifty seats. Very small, but very smart. Empty the night of the murder—that is, no production scheduled for it. Separated from Main Stage, the larger auditorium, by a narrow backstage corridor. The Main Stage production was *Taming of the Shrew*, known familiarly to theatre people as *Shrew*. Lots of running around in *Shrew*, lots of yelling and carrying on. Lots of sound cover in other words. Planned that way by a knowing murderer? Maybe, maybe not.'

'You left out that she was raped.'

'Yeah,' Jacob said.

Cox studied him. 'Bruises, clothes mussed and torn, semen traces . . .?'

'Who's arguing? ME says rape, so rape it is. I mean, this is Doc Pettibone we're talking about, one of the true forensic geniuses of our time. Still, wasn't it Pettibone who once did a PM on a fifteen-year-old male who turned out to be a fourteen-year-old female?'

'There were extenuating circumstances.'

'What were they?'

'Are you saying it wasn't rape?'

'No.'

'You're saying it could have been rape, but that some element deep in the Horowitz psyche has become alive to other possibilities.'

'Is that what I'm saying? Maybe so.'

'But you're allowing the fact of a sex act.'

'Oh yeah.'

'So our murderer either raped and killed her, or made love to her and killed her. Does it matter?'

'Not to her. Maybe not even to us. At least not yet.'

Cox nodded. 'Last person to see her alive was the doorman at her office building, right?'

'Last person we know of. He saw her leave around half past seven, quarter of eight. Anyway before eight, he says. It's a five-minute walk from her office to the theatre if you cut through the Jessup Street Mall.'

After a moment Cox said, 'The word is Judge Duncannon was not a theatre-lover.'

'That's what I hear.'

'In fact, except for special occasions, she seldom went near the place.'

'First nights—and only then if Tait was appearing.'

'So . . .?'

Jacob waited.

'What the hell was she doing in that empty dressing-room with her husband out of town?'

'Maybe she didn't know he was out of town. Tait himself isn't sure she did. Anyway the room wasn't exactly empty. Somebody was there to bruise her.'

'And boff her.'

Jacob considered possible sequences. Bruise her and boff her, or boff her and bruise her? Where was tenderness? And where was the sequence that with bruising and boffing in the picture would account for a casually discarded or perhaps a not so casually discarded .22? Spider mite responses began to form, but he turned away from them disdainfully as premature and therefore undisciplined.

'For what it's worth,' he said, 'the blood group matched by those semen traces is AB.'

'*Is* it worth anything?'

'Not so far.'

'Could be, though. Only ten per cent of the population is Type AB. What type's Tait?'

'AB.'

That pleased Cox. He gave Jacob a knowing glance. 'Tell me again about that alleged lost weekend of his.'

'He had himself stashed in his mountain hideaway. No phone, no TV or radio, nothing. Alone with *Hamlet*.'

'Who's Hamlet? His dog?'

Jacob looked at him.

'Yeah, yeah, I know who Hamlet is. Why'd he want to be alone with *it*?'

'It's his next production. He wanted to concentrate, no distraction. *Hamlet*'s not like *Shrew*, he says. Whenever he does *Hamlet* he goes off and lives with it until he gets his idea about it. Tuesday morning, on his way home, he stopped for breakfast and saw a newspaper.'

'You believe all that?'

'He's persuasive.'

'Persuasive? The son of a bitch is an actor, for God's sake.'

'Yeah,' Jacob said, acknowledging. 'Acting is the art of the artful lie. I read that somewhere once.'

They considered the implications of this. Lies, they both knew, were staples of a homicide case. Experienced police officers went into an investigation prepared to encounter nothing but—and not merely first degree lies, those generated by the guilty in behalf of guilty hides. There were the second or third degree lies as well, those generated by the innocent (at least legally) to protect others. But experienced police officers made use of lies. Often it was their skill at isolating these that began the unravelling process. So what they didn't need was someone likely to be as good at lying as they were at isolating.

Cox lifted his personalized bullet-cum-paperweight. He examined it not with his customary blend of affection and pride, but with 'headline murder' vexation. He then slammed it down on the desk again, honouring the cherry-wood with yet another distinctive scar.

'Hate actors,' he said. 'Hate and despise them. And if you ask me Sunday Square is a damnfool place to put a theatre, ten-twelve blocks from the heart of town.'

'People find it,' Jacob said.

'Nothing but churches there once,' Cox said. 'Used to be *my* church, damn it. Blessed Mary.' He mumbled something in which the phrase 'murder *and* heresy' was audible. Then: 'Tait, the son of a bitch. There's your man. *His* wife, *his* dressing-room. *His* semen, for God's sake. He boffed her, then busted her. I feel it in my bones . . . you're not the only one with intuition. You listen to me, Jacob. No society worth a damn ever trusted its actors. That's what *my* old grandfather used to say. Never turn your back on an actor. They eat your food, drink your liquor, and steal your women.'

Jacob took the commentary under advisement. 'Does it matter that he doesn't seem to have a motive?' he asked after a moment. 'He liked her a lot, according to all reports. And she was dotty over him—Second Space was her birthday present to him, for instance. Unless what you're telling me is he's a psychopath.'

'You never heard of John Wilkes Booth?'

Jacob confessed that he had.

'My money's on the actor,' Cox said.

'I talked again to the ad agency tycoon,' Jacob said. 'And to his wife. And to Neil Duncannon, too, of course. None of them could shed any light on what the judge was doing in Tait's dressing-room that night.'

'Or saw her there.'

'No one saw her there.'

'No one admits having seen her there,' Cox said, a leaf from Jacob's book.

'Alibis? The actor can prove he was at his mountain hideaway?'

'No. But his stage manager verifies that he called Friday at about six, saying he wouldn't be at the theatre that night.'

'He wasn't in . . .' Pause. Now with disdainful emphasis. '*Shrew?*'

'He directed it, but he wasn't appearing in it. Still, he did have to cancel an audition he'd scheduled. With a talented amateur named Margaret Duncannon. At Second Space.'

'Pull him in, Jacob. Do yourself a favour. Pull him in and sweat him. If it don't mean all that much now, it will by the time you're through with him. Actors. Nothing but shells. Everybody knows that. Sweat him, and he'll crack wide open.'

Jacob tapped a bicuspid, but did not seem otherwise primed for action.

After a moment Cox said, 'Does Alec Duncannon have an alibi?'

'All the Duncannons have alibis. In fact three of them have the same one. Alec and Margaret were having dinner at Karen Duncannon's apartment. The party didn't break up until around half past eleven.'

'And the kid brother spent the night with that Amy Ashbogen, lucky young bastard.'

'It's just actors you hate? Actresses are OK?'

'That one is.'

Both then lapsed into thoughtfulness—Cox toying with his bullet, Jacob with the disquieting notion that whereas it might be convenient to go sniffing after Duncannons, the fact was that they barely scratched the surface of those who were on less than pleasant terms with the defunct judge.

Cox leaned forward, pointing the bullet at Jacob with transparent symbolism. 'Nobody saw her, nobody heard her, how the hell did she get in?'

'She had a key. We found it on her. A lot of people have keys, Tait says. He gives them out freely. Theatre's not nine to five, he says. Between Main Stage and Second Space he's got something going on virtually non-stop. If it's not a performance, then it's a workshop, or auditions, or a class. And so people need access. Early on, he says, he decided not to worry about getting ripped off. And by and large he hasn't been.'

'He'll come in one day and find fifty seats around a hole in the ground. And it'll serve him right.'

'Funny thing about the judge's key, though,' Jacob said.

'What?'

'Couldn't get Tait to actually say he gave her one.'

The bullet slipped from Cox's fingers and buried itself in his wastepaper basket. It was not easy to recover. Advertising circulars, the Wall Street *Journal*, and orange peels appeared on the vinyl flooring—and eventually the bullet. Order restored, Cox said, 'Maybe she went looking for twenty bucks in Tait's pocket one night, found his keys, and had a duplicate made.'

'Why would she do that?'

Cox had meant it as a joke, but a glance at Jacob's narrowed eyes and distant expression made him ask, 'Why *would* she do that?'

'Maybe it wasn't twenty bucks she was looking for. Maybe it was something else.'

'What?'

'I don't know. Maybe the keys to Second Space, so she could have a duplicate made.'

'You think so?'

Jacob shrugged. He got up.

'Where are you going?'

'Not sure. But somewhere. If I don't, first thing you know Knudsen'll be back, see me sitting around, and you'll be in trouble for not kicking my ass in gear.'

Jacob was at the door when Cox called his name. 'Remember a certain hard-nosed black guy named Slidell?' he asked.

'You know I do. Boss of the local FBI. Why?'

'Been around asking questions.'

'About Judge Duncannon?'

'Uh-uh,' Cox said. And then, not without a degree of perverse pleasure, added: 'About you.'

## CHAPTER 2

The address was unimpressive, the building indistinguished, and the office itself predictably commonplace, but Helen had not yet reached the point where she could turn the key without a sense of excitement. Her desk, her troika of chairs—never mind that none of them matched—her framed photographs (of Jacob and Timmy, her son), her 'Scenes of the Great Southwest' calendar, her vibrant Apache rug mounted on one of the walls, her this and her that, her *business*.

And her business for a full year. Jacob had not only promised but insisted.

'Give yourself a shot. What's money for?'

And so they had cashed in the junk bonds and two of the mutual funds.

'Jacob,' she had said on D-Day minus one, 'are you sure?' She waved her letter of resignation at him.

He had folded her into a bear hug. 'You think Sam Spade wasn't scared first week on the job?'

And so here she was. And though still intact, so to speak, after more than a month, no longer much worried. She knew why, too. In part Jacob and the reassurance he could always deliver. But also the Apache in her, manifested at times like this in a calming fatalism. It descended after a while and made it possible for her to sit her spotted pony and wait for hours. Either the deer would water or they would not.

A knock at the door. Her heart took an un-Apache-like leap. In the wake of the knock appeared Neil Duncannon, and her heart settled at once to its comfortable trot. He noticed the cause and effect of this. Whatever he made of it amused him, but he kept the joke to himself.

'Nice,' he said, glancing about him.

'If you're partial to closets.'

'Don't kid me, Helen Horowitz. You love it.'

She grinned. 'Cup of coffee?'

'No, thanks.'

'Stronger?'

He raised a brow. 'You've got the PI's obligatory bottle of Old Something in the bottom drawer?'

'And clean glasses in the other drawer.'

'I'll pass for now.' He took one of the unmatched chairs. 'This is not a social call. I am about to latch on to your professional services, so no booze until we've come to terms.'

His tone was flip, it almost always was. But something underlying sent a signal, and she looked at him again. When she did she came alert. Like all good-looking people, he found it relatively easy to camouflage trouble: observers so seldom expected him to have any. Still, Helen had known and liked him for going on three years, long enough to have learned wariness. Now she could spot it when the warm brown gaze and the good wide grin were just that touch unsynchronized. In the subtlest of ways it was as if gaze and grin belonged to separate but equal faces.

'Speak,' she said.

He squinted down at his hands. 'A tale of woe. It may not sound that way at first, but hang in there.'

She waited.

'Guess who sent for me yesterday morning. No, don't guess that. Guess this. Who did my sister leave her money to?'

'If you hadn't put it just that way I would have guessed her husband, of course. Wrong?'

'Wrong.'

By now the answer had become obvious, though startling notwithstanding. 'My goodness,' she said.

'Yes,' he said. 'It's likely to come as a surprise to quite a few folk, isn't it?'

'It's certainly going to surprise Jacob. He thought the husband was a lock.'

He was silent.

'For the record, she left her money to you?'

'All but a shred or two, according to Lawyer Linderman.'

'Was there a lot?'

'A sufficiency. You're looking at a rich man.'

'Now I think you better tell me when this becomes a tale of woe.'

He got up from the chair and went over to study her Police Academy diploma and her two COPs: Certificates of Oustanding Performance. Though he lingered before the one personalized by Mayor Knudsen with a handwritten note, she knew he hadn't read a single stirring word.

Resuming his seat, he said, 'It seems my girl has had her fill of the moneyed class. The former Mrs Grant, in case you've forgotten.'

'Amy Ashbogen,' she said. 'I haven't forgotten.'

Amy Ashbogen. It was a name that meant a little something to her. They had never met, but Helen liked remembering the first time she had seen her perform: a pivotal part though in a not very good Off Broadway period piece about the ante-bellum South. The leading man had been an old-stager. And compulsive up-stager. Repeatedly, during the first act, he had found pieces of business to do Amy in. Helen, up front, had taken more interest in the progress of their contest than she had in the legitimate drama. Finally, late in the second act, during an embrace, one of his arms snaked around to cover the left side of Amy's mouth just as she was about to score with her curtain speech. Helen had edged forward a bit. There was a one beat pause. Then, lifting the hand away, Amy sent the line soaring to the last row of the balcony, after which she carefully put the hand back in place. Tremendous burst of laughter and applause. Deeply satisfied, Helen had relaxed in her seat.

'I love watching her,' she said. 'She's clever. And of course she'd got that marvellous voice. And big role, small role, she goes for what she can, doesn't she?'

He smiled. 'That's my baby.'

'Is your baby something of a crackpot?'

'Because she's not bowled over by a pisspot full of money? Would you be if you didn't like the strings attached?'

'But the strings in this case are you.'

'Yes. Well, maybe that's the point.' Once more he was on his feet, trekking to the literature on her walls, perusing it all blindly. He turned. 'Go and talk to her,' he said.

'Me?'

'Let me rephrase that. I want to *hire* you to go and talk to her. You understand? In your professional capacity.'

'I don't think that's what private investigators do, Neil.'

'How do you know? You're still only a short-termer. Come on, we'll structure it any way you want. By the hour, as a project . . . you forget how rich I am.'

'Why me anyway?'

'Because she'll like you. I'm absolutely certain she will. And you'll like her.'

'I had my lip split once by someone who was absolutely certain to like me. What would I be talking to her about?'

'Me.'

'That much I guessed. To what end? What would my objective be?'

'Whatever's possible. It's like with an ad sometimes. Sometimes there's no real message, but it's important to keep your name before the public.'

'Couldn't you do that as well as I could?'

'I thought I told you—I'm banished.'

'Banished? What do you mean, banished?'

'Her first reaction was—Goodbye, Neil, clean breaks are best. Banished came later, as a reduced sentence.'

'For how long?'

'She makes no promises.' He crossed the room to her, placed his hands on her shoulders and shook her gently. 'Helen, do this for me, please. Right now, I'd say my chances are seventy-thirty against. She loves me. I think she loves me. I even think *she* thinks she loves me. But if it's a matter of principle—or anything in that country—I'm dead. That's the way she is.'

Helen cleared her throat a couple of times, an exercise meant to tune the brain as well as the vocal cords. But when she was ready to speak he stopped her.

'I *know* what you're going to say. It's going to be wise as hell and a total waste of breath. On the upside, it's going to have to do with all my shiny new options, on the downside with Judge Grant's mysterious connections. and maybe in between you'll do a fast few minutes on the nature of infatuation and the tons of absurdities generated in its name by lovesick fools like me.' He took her hands. 'Please don't bother.'

'You think you're smart, don't you?'

He squeezed the hands he was holding.

'I'll think about it,' she said.

'The other thing I want you to do *professionally* is keep an eye on the house. Open my mail, stuff like that, so if my party drafts me to run for president I'll know about it. Bill me heavy for that and throw in a visit—maybe two visits—to Amy as incidentals. Deal?'

'I said I'll think about it.'

'I'm leaving in the morning.'

'Neil, this . . . windfall. It was a complete surprise?'

'Nothing Ellie did could ever be a complete surprise.' Dry smile. 'It wasn't even a complete surprise to Wiley.'

'Why not?'

He looked at her. 'Do you have a specific interest in this? Or are you just glancing over Jacob's shoulder? Don't bother to answer. In either case you'd have to consult Wiley.'

'Did you?'

'What?'

'Consult him.'

'I'm not sure I know what you mean.'

'Have you been in touch with him?'

'I called to commiserate. And to—' He broke off.

Intuitive flash. 'And to offer him a piece of the pie? How big a piece? All?'

'Actually, I called to make sure he didn't think I'd been conspiring. Wiley's a friend I couldn't bear to lose.'

'I bet you didn't. Lose him, I mean.'

'No.'

'Did he accept your idiotic offer?'

'No.'

She smiled. 'Nobody could easily think of you as a conspirator. An idiot but never a conspirator.'

'One visit? And maybe a follow-up phone call? *Please?*

'Go,' she said, a dramatic finger indicating the door. 'I got out of the juvenile delinquency business because I didn't want to deal any more with people of your ilk.'

He shuffled his feet, but only in part as a joke. It was clear he yearned for commitment.

'Now,' she said firmly. 'This minute. I'll call you tonight.'

## CHAPTER 3

You could see how bulky he might have been in his prime, a period that had passed some fifty years ago if you pegged a man's prime at, say, forty. Phillip Linderman was now ninety-one. He was still tall, big-chested, and reasonably straight, but when Jacob helped him off with his raincoat he realized how twiglike the arms were. They felt breakable. Jacob found himself exercising great care.

While Jacob hung the coat in the closet, the young woman

guided the old man into the swivel chair behind the desk. It was a huge leather chair, pock-marked with holes. There were also slashes, welts and cracks. It was a thoroughly disreputable chair, and Jacob decided people had spent the past few years trying to wrest it from Mr Linderman. No way. He would defend it tigerishly. Likewise the battle-scarred old desk, yin to the chair's yang.

Jacob guessed the young woman was Sybil Linderman.

'You haven't been waiting long, have you?' she asked.

'Five minutes or so.'

'Something came up. I . . . I'm sorry, but there was nothing I could do about it.'

Linderman cackled. 'She thought I was having a heart attack, that's what came up. Wouldn't listen to me when I told her I *know* the difference between a heart attack and indigestion. Why wouldn't I? Had two of the big buggers already. You ever had a heart attack, young feller?'

'No, sir.'

He glanced at Jacob measuringly, as if to calculate how far in the future his myocardial infarction might be. But if a conclusion was reached it was not reported. 'Anyway, she drags me willy-nilly into a goddam cab, and we go a block and a half and turn right around. Ten hard-earned cash dollars out the window.'

'If you'd let me call an ambulance—'

'Over my dead body.' That struck him as funny. He walloped the table gleefully and then extended a rapier-like finger Jacob's way. 'Heard about the latest development?'

'Yes. Miss Linderman called me. That's—'

But now the finger slashed at her. 'Who said *you* should call him?'

She kept silent. She was a tall, slender woman in her early thirties with dark hair and very pale skin. Her hair was sensibly combed. Everything about her was sensible: clothes, shoes, glasses. Except for the power legs, which were much too long and shapely to be thought of as sensible.

And slash and waggle though it would, the finger failed to slice from her a sliver of composure.

'Last night you asked me to call Lieutenant Horowitz first thing this morning,' she said.

'Like hell.'

'Then I must have been mistaken,' she said, without turning a sensible hair.

He glared. Then, swiftly as it had come, the anger faded. His eyes were old but surprisingly lively, and now he managed a sort of milky-blue twinkle. 'Smart,' he said to Jacob. 'Smartest young lawyer in this building full of hot-shot young lawyers, Miss Sybil is. Harvard. Top of her class. Don't *come* much smarter, and she knows it. Pay no mind to that goody-goody crap. Got that from her mother. Got her brains from her father. And that's *me* in case you were wondering, sonny. Sixty-five when I caught her sixteen-year-old ma in a Kansas cow-barn and rammed her good. Knocked her up, had to marry her, shotgun style.'

Jacob could not help the glance he flicked at Miss Linderman.

Her face remained expressionless.

'Don't look at her. You'll only get the gussied-up version from her.'

'No, he wouldn't, Father. He'd get your version.' Slight smile. 'Only I might not have volunteered it.' Pause. 'But you're here about Duncannons not Lindermans, aren't you, Lieutenant?'

'Yes. How well did you know the judge?'

'Not very,' she said. 'My father—'

'Knew her better than just about anyone else in the world, including what *you'd* call her family. Knew her better than the husband, better than the brothers, better than that fool, her father, or that slut, her mother. Ellie clerked for me, goddammit. She . . .' A thought, a stab of regret, or something perhaps too vague for definition, made him wince and then was gone. Jacob wondered if he'd even been aware of it. 'Liked her, too,' the old man said. 'Nobody else did, but I did. She was honest, plumb honest—the way they don't come any more. She couldn't stand crooks, couldn't stand to be on the same planet with them, couldn't stand their stink.' He paused to let his breath escape in a tea-kettle whistle. 'Liked her a whole lot better than Dorian Gray over there in the corner office.'

Jacob looked at Miss Linderman who, somewhat reluctantly, said, 'Judge Grant.'

Once more the old man's finger stabbed, this time with the absent judge as target.

'Sneak into his office some night and you'll find this cruddy portrait stashed away in some closet. Goddam thing looks older than me.'

Jacob, vastly interested, waited for more, looking forward to an indiscretion or two. He had no idea what form these might take, but Richard Grant was an evocative figure, the kind that could add dimension to a case badly in need. But the old eyes had been busy, and the old man now subsided into an amused silence. Jacob wondered what would happen if he stretched the silence. Would Linderman spill? How tough was nonagenarian resolve? Two minutes passed, and the old man slapped the desk again, cackling loudly, after which he reached into a drawer to drag out a nail file. He began to hum and trim. Jacob looked at Miss Linderman and saw her slight smile again. He decided *everybody* knew what he was up to and knocked it off.

'Judge Duncannon was supposed to have adored her husband,' he said. 'Then, just like that, he's disinherited. Was all of Tri-Towns wrong?'

'It usually is,' Linderman said.

'Did *you* think Judge Duncannon adored her husband?'

'Mighty interesting what he thought, wasn't it, Sybil? Though we ain't about to tell it to any policeman. Ever hear of confidentiality, Policeman?'

'When did she change her will?' Jacob asked.

'Last Friday.'

'The very day of her death?'

The old man grinned.

'I wonder why you waited all this time—'

Walloping the desk like a jazz band drummer, Linderman said, 'My business, not yours. Nobody's business but mine who I tell what to when.'

Jacob thought Miss Linderman looked as if she might have wanted to amend that, but she kept silent.

'How long before the change did you guess it was on the way?' Jacob asked.

'Confidential, confidential.'

'Come on now, Mr Linderman, your client's dead. And what I'm trying to find out is why. And then eventually who. Confidentiality has limits, doesn't it?'

Half way through this Jacob decided he stood a better chance if he addressed the speech to the daughter and turned in that direction. The father answered anyway.

'Hell it does, hell it does,' he said, jumping up and down as if his seat had gone infra red.

'Father . . .' Clearly, it was a warning.

'Confidentiality, conf—'

Motioning to Jacob, she moved swiftly out of the office. He followed unquestioningly. (Later it occurred to him to wonder a bit about that.) To the middle aged-woman with blue hair at the reception desk—already on her feet and waiting command—she said, 'He'll have his warm milk now, Annie.' She then cut across the corridor to the large office facing her father's, Jacob in her wake.

'He loves an audience,' she said, shutting the door behind him. 'It was his great strength as a lawyer, and I've often thought he would have made a splendid actor. But sometimes when he gets over-excited we simply have to isolate him. I know how insensitive it must seem, walking out on him as if he were suddenly a pariah—still, we've systematized it, you see, and it's effective. I remove the audience,

Miss MacPherson moves in instantly and sits with him while he sips his milk. This quiets him. By the time he's finished the milk he's forgotten what it was that excited him, and he's in a mood to return to work. Incidentally, you'd be amazed at the amount he can do. He used to have an enormous trial practice. These days he confines himself to wills, but the quality of whatever he produces is still impeccable.' She paused, glanced at Jacob ruefully and then said, 'Except he misplaces things now and again.'

'Judge Duncannon's will?'

She nodded.

Jacob took stock. Except for a slim vase containing three yellow gladioli, her office was as spartan as her father's. The gladiolis were on the far corner of a desk carefully (Jacob would have bet) less impressive than its counterpart. The chair, too, was scaled down. The leather of course had the bloom of youth.

'My three o'clock is due shortly, Lieutenant,' she said, consulting her watch, 'and I must prepare for her. But I do want to know if there's a way I can be of service. As he made clear just now, my father liked Judge Duncannon a great deal, and she . . . revered him.'

Jacob tried one from the hip. 'You can tell me how come she was in that dressing-room last Friday night,' he said.

Her face revealed nothing. Watching it, however, gave Jacob the opportunity to decide he approved of it. It was a plain enough face, but it would take on interest with the years. Like her father's, it was made for durability. The Linderman eyes were noteworthy in her case, too—lively, livelier than he had at first believed. Still, it was no open book, that face. If it was a book at all, it was a diary, and she was not about to leave it around for strangers to read.

'I don't know,' she said. 'Judge Duncannon didn't confide in me. Father did her will, and on occasion I was present when they conferred, but that was pretty much the extent of our relationship.'

'You disliked her?'

'Oh no.'

'Why not? You wouldn't have been alone.'

She shrugged.

'All right, then, you'd describe your relationship as . . . what? Limited but cordial.'

'I respected her.' Dry smile. 'I also empathized with her. That is, I'm quite certain people say the same sort of thing about me they said about her: good legal brain, not much spark. Perhaps if we had known each other better, we might have been friends. At least, so I've thought since her death.'

'Why would she disinherit her husband?'

'I have no idea. I don't know him very well either, Lieutenant. I've only seen him twice in my life.'

Funny, the way sympathy could come from nowhere to link the unlikeliest men and women, Jacob thought, on discovering, suddenly, that it was operative between this woman and himself—a development, oddly enough, that seemed to have surprised neither of them. How explain it? Was sex the ever-constant first cause? He supposed so, in some Byzantine way, though here was certainly not the all-enveloping lust that had left him shivering one hot summer day in Helen Bly's office. The Apaches had a phrase for it, which Jacob could never quite recall. Connectedness, was Helen's over-simplified (for his benefit) translation. Connectedness now made it clear that Sybil Linderman wanted to be asked about Wiley Tait. So he did.

'On the stage was the first time,' she said. She took a moment.

It seemed to him now there was more colour in her face, that in some subtle way it had become younger.

'He filled it, the way big men of talent can. I saw him as *Othello*. He was brilliant. My father, who not only loves acting but truly understands it, once told me trust is at the heart of it, trust in oneself. I believe that. The point is, I trust nothing about myself, which is why I'm so dreadful in front of juries. But big men find it easy to trust their bodies, don't they? And that's a good place to start.' Dry smile reprised. 'Like you, Lieutenant. I mean, I think you're a good actor, too.'

Jacob decided to let that pass.

'The other time I saw him,' she said, 'was here, yesterday, for the reading of the will.'

'And what was remarkable about that?'

'He seemed . . . unmoved.' Unconsciously squinting as if to better focus an inner eye, she was silent a moment. 'Had you just walked into the room you might have thought he had inherited and Neil Duncannon been cut out.'

'Maybe the disinheriting didn't come as news to Tait? Is that possible?'

'Quite possible, I should imagine. And if true you'd be out of a suspect, wouldn't you?'

'Why?'

'Well, why would he kill to benefit someone else?'

He studied her. 'I think you want me to be without that suspect.'

Not much subtle about the flush that climbed from neck to temple now. It was deep red and swept everything in its path, but she said nothing. After a moment, Jacob, getting to his feet, said, 'Listen, thanks for your help. OK to get back to you later if I need to?'

'A crush at my age,' she said bitterly. 'You think I'm a fool, don't you?'

He had reached the door. He stopped, looked back at her, and tapped a bicuspid before he spoke. 'With me it's Brooke Shields,' he said. 'Damn near wrote her a letter once.'

'Did you?'

'On my thirty-ninth birthday.'

She smiled. He thought this time there was amusement in it.

*

Leaving the building, he saw a navy blue Caddie parked across the street, peering down its nose at the passing parade. Jacob was not a Caddie lover. Exceedingly long and deeply exhibitionistic, he thought this one. Pompous even for a Caddie. It was at rest in a no-parking zone. Three men occupied it. Two of them were white. These were carefully dressed in dark suits, blue and white striped shirts, red ties. The black man's clothes were not unlike theirs, but he sat behind them, overseeing them, as it were, in a way that emphasized something still rather new in socio-economic dialectics. Jacob recognized him at once: Slidell. As he crossed the street the two in front kept their gazes fixed on the windshield; Slidell, though, watched him every step of the way until he arrived.

'You have business with me?' Jacob asked.

Not an inch or a pound over average, Slidell was nevertheless one of those men conversations got quiet around. There was an aura. It seemed to say: I have never in my life been happy. I blame you for it. Bald, bony dome, thin nose and lips, an ugly knife scar which divided his right cheek jaggedly. Jacob knew the history of that scar. One of Jacob's sergeants, Art Hickman, had assisted at its birth. Hickman, bored and soporific at the tail-end of a summer afternoon, had been waiting, longer than he thought necessary, to arraign a murder suspect at the Tri-Town Courthouse. The suspect caught him in mid-yawn, shoved him over a bench, and ran for daylight, brandishing the knife previously concealed in his cowboy boot. Slidell happened to be entering as the suspect was exiting. Collision. As a result, Slidell received his lacerated cheek. Thirty seconds later, with the same knife, he cut the suspect's throat, just short of fatally. While Slidell was still in the Emergency Room, friends had put the case to Tri-Town's commissioner of police: flagrant carelessness, take the fuck-up sergeant's badge. Jacob had seen no choice but to intervene, citing a reasonably respectable six-year record to balance a single serious mistake.

Commissioner McCracken (benefiting for once from Captain Cox's counsel) took the stripes but not the badge. Slidell's comment to Jacob: 'Maybe you owe me one.' Ten months ago that had been. Icy stares when they met, but the Tri-Towns took in enough territory to make the rate of frequency bearable.

He invited Jacob to join him in the Caddie. Jacob did. The flunkeys in front did not turn as the glass that split the car into Upstairs/Downstairs slid into place. Slidell said, 'Now everything's between us girls.'

'And whatever bugs you've planted.'

'Why would I want a bug for a conversation with you?'

'You'd want a bug for a conversation with your mother.'

Slidell studied him. Jacob studied back. And while they were thus matriculating the Caddie got underway. 'Taking you for a ride, Horowitz. Ain't you scared?'

Slidell's skin was blue-black. His smile was darker.

'Tell those pederasts in the front seat to stop this ash-can,' Jacob said.

'Why?'

'I'm getting out.'

'You don't like the way I talk to you?'

'There's that, and I hate Cadillacs.'

Slidell leaned back in his seat and was so still that for a moment Jacob thought he had fallen asleep. Then, with his eyes closed, he said, 'Man, they'd have to drag you out of here with a billygoat rope.'

'How come they would?'

'Because you're dyin' to know what's going down.'

Jacob kept silent.

At the end of an æon or so, Slidell said, 'Maybe you better tell me about you and the judge.'

'Never saw her in my life. Alive, that is.'

'Not that judge. The judge I'm interested in is the one you played tennis with.'

Jacob stared at him.

'Which one of those words is hard to understand?' Slidell asked.

'All of them.'

'So OK, let's us take it again. You listening good now? The Federal Bureau of Investigation is interested. The United States Government is interested. Itty-bitty ol' me comes third.'

'That's a lot of heavy interest.'

'Yeah.'

'Is this the kind of game where if I'm interesting to you, when it's your turn you get interesting to me?'

'It might be.'

Again they studied each other, Jacob tapping a bicuspid, Slidell caressing his scar. Then: 'Go,' Slidell said.

'What I know for sure about Judge Grant is he's Main Line Philly with upper-crust credentials on both sides. Snooty-folk, Slidell, if you know what I mean.'

'Yeah, my folk picked cotton for dem folk.'

'And my folk sold dem folk rags off pushcarts.'

Slidell seemed to smile.

'The old man was political,' Jacob said. 'In fact, Grants have been movers and shakers in Republican circles since *the* Grant, Lincoln's top gun. Richard is supposed to be descended, incidentally—a great great great-something or other. But much more to the point is the judge's ranking among eastern clay court tennis-players, which was pretty high one year. I figured that was the kind of talent might help me win a friendly grudge match. Outside of that I say hello to him when I see him, and he says hello to me. Over the years we've had lunch together twice and dinner once after having appeared on some TV panel show. Probably fair to say we find each other good company. Blink an eye if you're still awake.'

Slidell got both eyes functional and stared at Jacob stonily.

'What I *hear* about Grant is something else again,' Jacob said, 'but that's strictly rumour.'

'What rumour?'

'You know damn well what rumour.'

'Tell me.'

Jacob shrugged. 'That for him gambling is the Big G. Like heroin's the Big H for other types. And that to support his habit he's had to become a friend of the Family.'

Again Slidell seemed to have gone to sleep. Jacob waited.

'There was a wire on Judge Duncannon,' Slidell said. 'We put it there.'

Jacob whistled.

'*Her* idea,' Slidell said.

'You're telling me you recruited—'

Slidell held up his hand. 'She came to us—to me—two and a half months ago. There are common pleas judges on the take, she said. More than a few, she thought. But one she was dead certain of, she said, was Richard Grant.'

'I don't believe it.'

Slidell went to sleep again.

Jacob embroidered his whistle with a colourful little trill. 'But that's amazing,' he said. 'A judge willingly puts a wire on against another judge? That's goddam unheard of.'

Slidell shrugged.

'Come on, Slidell, you *know* it's amazing. Talk about your closed corporations. What's more closed than judges?'

'Told us she felt personally disgraced. Told us bent judges were the rotten apples that had to be got out of the barrel.'

Jacob fed the information into his computer and let it whirr around a bit. 'She *was* a one for moral outrage, they say.'

'I'd do the same,' Slidell said. 'I mean, if it was my barrel. So would you, they say.'

'Anything turn up on the tape?'

'A couple of promising moments, nothing real good. But you had a feeling it was heading in the right direction.'

For awhile they were both silent. Then Slidell said, 'What was she doing in that dressing-room?'

'Get in line. Everybody's favourite unanswered question. Here's one for you. Where was Grant that Friday night?'

'You don't know?'

'Up until like thirty seconds ago I didn't think I needed to know,' Jacob said.

'In Philly. Some kind of big-shot charity jamboree with tuxes, and it takes five hundred to buy a ticket.'

'And five hundred people willing to swear they saw him there,' Jacob said.

'Why not? He *was* there,' Slidell said.

Jacob nodded. Then: 'Neil Duncannon told me his sister asked him to deliver a package for her earlier that afternoon. He wouldn't. You think she might have gone instead?'

'And that's how come she was in that dressing-room?'

'Yeah,' Jacob said.

'What kind of package?'

'A package.'

'Deliver to who?'

'A package, that's all he knows.'

'You believe him?'

'Yeah,' Jacob said.

'Maybe it was this package guy who did it to her,' Slidell said.

'Lots and lots of maybes,' Jacob said.

'Yeah, and maybe you could talk to someone,' Slidell said.

'Who?'

'Someone from your old neighbourhood.'

And then of course Jacob was clued in. Salvatore Crowley, now a highly placed *capo*, had spent his puberty and adolescence at 5524 Marwood Place. During many of those years Jacob had resided at 5523.

'I haven't seen Sal in six months,' Jacob said. 'He's had some bad things happen to him, which you probably know about. He went abroad to recover.'

'He's back,' Slidell said.

'You think Sal is Grant's Family connection?'

'One, I don't say he *is* connected. Two, if the habit was smack, or women, probably I'd be thinking some other connection. Anyway, all I say is talk to Sal the pal. They say he loves you.'

'Have *you* talked to Grant?'

'Got nothing to talk to him about. Yet.'

'But you're watching him.'

Slidell nodded, then let his fingers do the walking down the crooked path on his face. 'Whatever happened to Sergeant Hickman?' he asked.

Jacob crossed his arms on his chest.

'They say he resigned,' Slidell said.

'They tell *me* he was counselled into resigning. They tell me Mayor Knudsen called him in one morning and gave him good counsel.'

'With all his faults, the mayor ain't the dumbest man I ever knew. Hickman . . . maybe he just wasn't meant for law and order.'

Slidell knocked on the glass, and Jacob, who hadn't been paying attention, now saw that he was across the street from the precinct. The car stopped. Among Slidell's features there was a mustering that could have been on behalf of a grin. 'Fact is,' he said, 'you don't think that fat slug was any damn good either.'

Jacob got out.

It wasn't precisely that Doc Pettibone was stupid or dishonest. It was more that he was mean-spirited. He was a short, dark, scowling man who recoiled from much in life and two aspects of it in particular: (1) large people, (2) admitting error. Pettibone was Tri-Town Homicide's

Medical Examiner. And forensic expert. He was also an insurance doctor and a health education teacher for two private schools at opposite ends of the county. He was chronically busy. Which probably accounted for his compulsion to do things quickly. Which, in turn, probably accounted for a rather cursory approach to scene-of-the-crime examinations. 'Mind your own goddam business,' is a mild form of what he typically said to Nervous Nellies like Jacob when they hinted at the advisability of greater detail in his reports. Or, if he were feeling expansive: 'I'll pick it all up on autopsy.' Often he did. In Jacob's view, however, something better than often was a job requirement.

Six-five Jacob was not among Pettibone's favourites. Compounding the error of size, Jacob had in addition caught the ME in at least four shockers during the ten years of their association.

When the phone rang and he heard Pettibone's raspy, ill-natured voice Jacob was not unprepared to learn it heralded number five. And, as he had intimated to Cox, he also had a hunch as to what it might be.

'Jesus,' Pettibone said as preamble, 'how many pairs of hands do they think I've got? I can't do *everything* my goddam self. What am I, a goddam octupus?'

Jacob waited. At length Pettibone took a breath and said, 'Duncannon. I never liked that homo bitch when she was alive.'

'Funny, she thought the world of you.'

'Shut your ass, Horowitz, or I'll come over there and shut it for you.'

'When?'

'Now, if you want me to.'

'Give me an hour or so to say goodbye to Helen and get my affairs in order.'

That earned him two minutes of vitriol, ending in a violent coughing fit.

'All right, Doc. She *wasn't* raped?'

'How the hell did you know?'

'I didn't. It's just naturally the kind of thing you screw up.'

Beneath Pettibone's calumnification Jacob took stock of the new status quo. Rape *had* seemed wrong to him. He hadn't been able to tell Cox why, but rape had nagged at him and now he was relieved. Perhaps it was in the *way* her clothes had been torn—circumspectly; an effect, somehow, too studied? Or perhaps the real problem had been a mind-set about Ellie Duncannon, establishing ground rules for her victimization: you could murder her, yes; but not rape her. Foolish no doubt, but there it was. Go argue with the subconscious. At any rate he accepted the news unquestioningly.

Pettibone was going on about the callowness of a young, untried assistant and notations on the 'stiff sheet' that had been fed by mistake into the shredder. When Jacob heard the words 'no sign of forcible entry' he returned the phone to its cradle.

But he did not leave his desk right away. He sat there, thinking. Five minutes later he called back.

'You son of a bitch, you hung up on me,' Pettibone said. 'Who the hell do you think you are? Nobody hangs up on me. Nobody, you understand? I've got a mind to—'

'Doc,' Jacob said. Just the one word unadorned, without much in the way of tonal quality, not harsh or sharp or loud, or even tinged with threat, and yet air went hissing from the Pettibone balloon.

Almost diffidently: 'What?'

'Can you tell me how long between the time she had sex and time of death?'

'No. I might have been able to once, but that's the data that was on the goddam stiff sheet. Which the goddam genius fed to that goddam machine. Jesus, how am I supposed to run a—'

Jacob hung up again.

## CHAPTER 4

It happened as it always did. Something woke her—perhaps a sound, perhaps a piece of a dream. She never knew. But there she was upright and sweating. And remembering that other night the year before, that terrible night. An intruder; Jacob already in pursuit; gunfire; Jacob's hoarse cry, the noise of him falling, and the ragdoll look of him sprawled motionless at the bottom of the staircase. She shuddered. Who could have believed the injuries would turn out to be minor: a harmless shoulder wound and a torn Achilles tendon, both mended now without a trace. It was she who bore the post-operative scars. Scars? More like a kind of psychological neuralgia. On certain nights it gripped hard, causing sleeplessness and suffering.

Jacob slept on soundly.

She went downstairs for warm milk. And it was then, on her way to the kitchen, that she found Neil's note slipped under the door.

> Dearest Helen,
>
> When you read this, I'll be well on my way.
>
> Which means of course you don't get a chance to say no. (Tricky devil, that Neil Duncannon.)
>
> But you wouldn't have anyway. Not you. Not when a fella really needs a friend.
>
> Adoringly,
> Neil

As she finished, Jacob entered the kitchen, blinking and scratching. He looked at her, decided babying would be therapeutic and hugged and rocked gently. 'Know what my old grandfather used to say about a nightmare?'

'No.'

'Just a horse of another colour.'

She kept silent.

'He was very old at the time,' Jacob said. 'And not as funny as he once had been.'

She handed him Neil's note, and he read it. 'Damn right he's a tricky devil, I'm thinking.'

'And what else?' she asked.

'What what else?'

'You've got that hooded you-can't-fool-a-Horowitz look. Something in that note bothers you. Out with it.'

He took the note from her and read it again. 'Why doesn't he tell you where he's going? If your mission's successful, how are you supposed to call him home?'

'Maybe she calls him home.'

'Maybe.'

'What else? There *is* something else, I can tell.'

'Somebody murdered his sister,' Jacob said. 'And yet when he hires a private eye it's to intercede with his girl. And babysit his house. That's OK. I'm not saying there's anything wrong with that. But nothing about his sister's killer? Why not?'

'He didn't particularly like his sister.'

'He hated her?'

'No,' Helen said. 'Not hated.'

'So?'

'So maybe he thinks the murder part of it's already in capable hands, your hands, Jacob. In Grampa Horowitz's book of homilies I bet there's something about too many cooks.'

Jacob nodded. 'All right, I've decided to be persuaded for now.'

'Jacob . . .'

'What?'

'If Neil *had* hired me for the murder part . . .?'

He kissed her nose, then each of her eyes. 'We're a team, no?'

'Yes,' she said.

She made her ears accessible, on which he bestowed a blend of bites and kisses. And said, 'We've always been a team, right?'

She showed him the place at the base of her throat, and he kissed that, too. 'And we always will be a team?'

By then her knees had buckled and his were shaky, still they teamed up and somehow managed to climb the stairs and reach their bed.

Later he said, 'When you go check out Neil's house I'd like to go with you.'

'Why?'

'A hunch. Comes under the heading of not leaving stones unturned.'

'I don't think so, Jacob,' she said after a moment.

'You don't think so?'

'Not without a warrant.'

He got up on an elbow and stared at her. 'What happened to we're a team.'

'*You* said that, Jacob.' She burrowed into him. 'But I think it was mostly because you were randy.'

## CHAPTER 5

Whatever could be brightly painted had been treated that way, but the square-rigged, mostly sandstone theatre retained aspects of its former churchiness—a split not without aptness, Helen always thought. Ducking out of the rain, she furled her umbrella and took shelter under the large sign that projected over the entrance. It was a very large sign, constructed in two segments. The top half, wooden, vibrantly red with vivid yellow lettering, identified the building and designated its function: WILEY'S THEATER IN

THE SQUARE. The bottom, plasterboard, announced the current and coming main stage productions: *The Taming of the Shrew* and *Hamlet*. But the grim, ungiving, hundred-year-old sandstone delivered a metaphysical message of its own: Never mind what's coming short term, sinners, consider what's *coming*.

Entering, Helen found herself in a cheerier world—a warmly lighted, walnut-panelled ante-room. She faced the ticket office. A pretty young woman with tightly wound honey-blonde braids sat behind its barred window, reading a paperback copy of *Hamlet*. In friendly, though slightly unfocused fashion, her eyes lifted to Helen, who stated her business. The young woman picked up the phone to ask for Amy Ashbogen. In the meantime Helen examined the photos on the wall. Several of them were of the impresario himself, of course. In one he was Torvald to Amy's Nora, a production Helen had seen and liked. How must it feel to have his kind of handsomeness, she wondered. To wake up every morning, see that image in the mirror and know that any addition or deletion would be no more than tampering. And would you worry a lot about time's ravages? Certainly you would. Unless you were far less plagued by vanity than the bulk of your species. Well, let's not foreclose that possibility, she instructed herself, since, in her view, cynicism was intellectually vulgar. Noting the good laugh lines in his face, she became more optimistic on his behalf.

'Amy's working with Wiley, in Second Space,' the young woman said, artlessly pleased to be on a first name basis with such luminaries. 'But you're to go right in. Do you know which door?'

'I think so,' Helen said, and made her way unerringly. As she started up the stairs the young woman called to her. 'I'm being nosey, I know. I mean, it's none of my business, but are you auditioning?'

Helen thought about it for a moment and then said, 'In a way.'

Except for the two people on the stage, the small, handsome auditorium—fifty seats (velvet covered, very comfortable) with the miniature proscenium thrust among them—was empty. Helen placed herself in the last row and leaned back luxuriously, delighted to be there. Empty theatres were aphrodisiacal, she decided, having to quell a desire to wriggle. But then the desk at the rear of the stage caught her eye. Aside from the actors, it was the only object there. She wondered if it had been moved from the dressing-room; if, in fact, it might be the desk Ellie Duncannon had fallen against. She thought it might be. That sobered her. Good, she told herself. You were becoming girlish.

Amy spotted her, signalled peremptorily for her to come forward. She obeyed. As she got close she saw how sharp was the rake of even this tiny stage and how its slant could distort perspective. She then understood something she had only thought she understood before—the true wickedness of deliberate *up*staging.

Amy squinted into the gloom. 'Mrs Horowitz?'

'Yes.'

Helen felt herself measured and decided upon. There was no way to tell if she'd been approved of. Amy's smile was warm. But that's what actors were good at, beaming at the public.

'Wiley, this is Helen Horowitz. Mrs Horowitz, Mr Tait.'

'I know,' Helen said. 'I've been here before, often.'

Wiley was squinting at her, too. 'Horowitz,' he said. 'I'll be meeting with someone of that name about an hour from now. I'll be meeting with him at police headquarters. Would you be related?'

'By marriage.'

'I see.' He turned to Amy. 'She doesn't look like fuzz's wife, does she?' Before Amy could answer, however, he was back to Helen: 'I hear he hates actors. Is that true?'

'Not in the least.'

'Well, then he makes an exception in my case. But I suppose that's because he thinks I'm also a murderer.'

Helen kept silent.

He stared at her unhappily. But then, seeming to lighten, he cast an expansive arm about Amy's slender shoulders and said, 'Come, Ophelia, my child, let's one last time to the business at hand.'

'Sit you, my lady,' Amy said as they moved upstage.

She sat. And watched Polonius counselling his daughter. Playing with princes is playing with fire, he cautioned, as Polonius had been cautioning for almost four hundred years. But this particular duo was an odd fit in the Shakespeare canon. They played the scene in a mixture of Elizabethan and contemporary English, with dollops of American slang thrown in at unpredictable intervals. To Helen it was lively, entertaining and curiously affecting. At a certain point she was lifted out of herself, transported from the theatre to a shadowy corner behind the door of her father's study, listening as he threatened to lock her older sister in her room—in chains, if need be. (This was two nights before she slipped by his security system to elope with the thoroughly decent boy he had characterized as a 'shiftless trifler').

*'I want that honeypot of yours kept out of sight, Ophelia. You take my meaning?'*

*'Yes, Father.'*

*Suddenly he shakes her hard. 'Damn it, I don't like the way you said that. I think you think you're the one female in the world who can mess with that royal son of a bitch and get away with it.'*

*'Get away with what, Father?'*

*'Ophelia!' A roar.*

*She wrenches free. And for the first time there is fire in her, too. 'He likes me. He really likes me. I know him, and you don't. You don't know either of us. How could you? You're too bloody old.'*

*Silence. His rage, bitten back, is more frightening in that state because you sense its quality and magnify its potential. When he speaks his tone is venomous. 'Think of it this way,' he says. 'You're on a plane, heading towards your Aunt Alice with whom you are scheduled to spend the rest of your life. In New Mexico. On the desert. A hundred miles from the nearest goddam Burger King.'*

*No response. Her expression remains stony. Still, you know somehow that she's been defeated. In a moment her shoulders quiver slightly, then slump. Perceptibly, the fight goes out of her, and there's not much doubt that it always will.*

They held the pose for a moment while Helen applauded lustily. 'Wonderful, wonderful.'

Wiley grinned. But then to Amy: 'Overstated?'

'I don't know,' she said. 'Everybody always wants Ophelia nice and mealy-mouthed. Maybe I found something useful, a bit of iron for her. How could it hurt? Maybe make her more interesting. Audience might feel it a bit more when she goes bananas. Let me think about it.'

He nodded. He took Helen's hand and kissed it. 'Actors never murder anyone,' he said. 'They leave all their aggression on the stage. May I tell your husband you believe that?'

'Wouldn't do you much good.'

'If it were true, I bet it would.' He grabbed his jacket, made a leg, Elizabethan-style, and was gone.

Amy smiled. 'Is it possible for a man to be better-looking than that?' she asked.

'I doubt it,' Helen said.

The two women looked at each other, and Helen guessed they just might be thinking along the same lines, which, in rough, was that for some reason neither felt in danger of being moved by Wiley Tait. Plus the extension of this, which was that the mystery of emotional attachment remained enduring and inexplicable.

Amy said, 'Would you like some coffee?'

Helen said she would, and Amy beckoned her to follow

upstage. Behind the scrim was a narrow passageway and across that twin black enamelled doors. *The Lady or the Tiger* flashed into Helen's mind when she saw that both were marked 'Actors' Space'. Amy pushed one open. Helen saw an excellently appointed dressing-room. It was much larger than she had expected, large enough to accommodate an ample double-bed. On this was a flamboyant red tartan spread and many pillows of different sizes and colours. Three thickish black rugs were scattered over most of the floor. There was an awkward, empty area ten feet or so to the left of the door. Helen thought it was desk-shaped.

'Wiley likes his amenities,' Amy said, smiling as Helen adjusted to what she felt certain was not standard for small theatre dressing-rooms. 'The other room's OK, too, though not as bravura. Fewer pillows on the bed and only a plain brown cover.'

There were two framed photographs on the dressing-table, and even from the doorway Helen had no trouble identifying them: Wiley's late wife in one; his late parents in the other. His parents, the movie stars, wore Elizabethan garb—relics of a film they had once been famous for—and looked young and terrifically romantic. His wife wore her robe and looked judgemental.

'Costume pictures,' Amy said wryly.

'Both?'

Amy shrugged. 'I guess that means I didn't care much for Ellie Duncannon. And I guess it also means I shoot my fat mouth off sometimes. Oh God, that's not the real reason you came by, is it? To pump me?'

'About what?'

'Them. Wiley and Ellie. If it is, you're wasting your time. The only thing I know about them—or that—is Wiley Tait wouldn't hurt a fly. Period. The end.'

Helen smiled. 'Neil and Neil alone,' she said. 'I swear.'

'OK,' Amy said after a moment, 'how do you want your coffee?'

Next to the bed a coffee-pot was working unobtrusively. Having solicited preferences, Amy set about satisfying them. Helen watched her. She moved so well—quick, efficient steps mingled with sudden, space-eating swoops. These, however, were not so much efficient as they were irrepressible. She wore cut-off jeans with a loose white sweatshirt bloused over and inscribed: 'Nothing like a Dane.' Coffee ready, she handed Helen's mug to her, pointed to a chair, and aimed herself at the bed, where she bulwarked her head with pillows and balanced her own mug on her belly. She looked very young and pretty. But close up, not the beauty she had always seemed from the tenth row. Helen considered that a plus. It made her more accessible, though what she said next was not chock full of positive overtones.

'Please tell me why you allowed Neil to drag you into this. You seem such a sensible woman.'

Helen was silent a moment. 'You do know he's paying me. That's not the answer, of course. At least not the whole answer, but it is a fact.'

'Sure it is. Neil wouldn't keep that a secret.' She grinned. 'Has it struck you how absolutely ridiculous this is? I mean, it's Miles Standish and Priscilla Alden updated with a wrinkle or two. Well, go ahead. Persuade me.'

'I think all he's hoping for, really, is to keep the case open.'

'I never said it wasn't.'

'Didn't you?'

'No.' But then she sat up and swung her feet over the edge of the bed. With her heels she beat out a complex little tattoo against the sideboard. 'He's very quick, isn't he, our Neil?' she said finally.

'He's got one of those funny minds.'

'Funny how?'

'The kind females like to think of as female. He picks up on things.'

A moment passed, during which the two women felt remarkably compatible.

'Did you know Judge Duncannon?' Amy asked.

'Only by reputation.'

'A bitch, a high-powered bitch. I suppose that's unfair as hell, given the accomplishment. But *I* think of her in terms of what she did to Neil when he was too little to fight back. Still, he loved her. At least I think he did, don't you?'

'Yes,' Helen said, then added: 'Probably more than he knows yet.'

'God, who could have—' Amy broke off and shook her head. 'Is your husband close to an answer?'

'That's another funny mind. Muddles along, muddles along, and then one bright morning he wakes so *full* of answers you can't stand him.'

'Neil thinks he's terrific.'

Helen nodded.

'Which is nothing next to what Neil thinks of you. He told me what you did for him the night his wife left.' She grinned. 'He also told me what you wouldn't do.'

Helen's face warmed. To change the subject she said, 'Neil might have been the last one Judge Duncannon spoke to. Aside from her killer, that is. How he must wish now he'd gone to her.'

Amy converted her feet to drumsticks again and then said, 'It isn't so much the inheritance, you see. Granted I've never been comfortable getting things without a certain amount of mortifying the flesh, but that's me, *my* problem. Neil's is . . . may I call you Helen? Selma Horowitz lives down the hall from Bertha Ashbogen in Philadelphia.'

'Yes. Helen of course.'

'Neil's a bad risk, I think. And that's the problem in a nutshell, Helen. A long time ago he fell in love with the idea of Duncannon, the Romantic Failure. He cosies up to it, wallows in it. It keeps him from having to do much. If you're going to fail, if you're always going to fail, I mean if it's written in the stars that way, why bother working up a sweat? Do you see?'

'Yes, but couldn't you have an impact there?'

'Could I? I'm not sure.'

'I'm guessing you could. If anyone could.'

'If anyone could. I notice you don't go whole hog. You're a careful woman, Helen Horowitz.'

'Funny, I never thought of myself that way. No, I don't think I am, particularly. If I were I probably wouldn't have married Jacob. I mean, I lived in this tiny southwestern mountain town all my life and *liked* it. And yet willy-nilly I left it to come east with a hulking New York know-it-all who had alienated at least three-quarters of the people I loved. I had a brother, five uncles, and an aunt all eager to tell me what a bad risk Jacob was.'

'But you didn't believe them.'

Helen was silent a moment. 'Yes, I think I did.'

Amy threw back her head and laughed. Helen found herself reacting to it with pleasure—but as if it were a performance. Fleetingly, she wondered if, in fact, it was. Sure it was, she decided, but so what. It was real, too. Amy was an actress, always would be. You could no more cut that out of her—and keep her alive—than you could a pound of flesh from near the heart. And what fool would want to? It was the actress in her that made her singular. And so likeable.

After a moment Amy said, 'As far as the money's concerned, the irony is I'd probably get used to it a lot faster than Neil would. Not in a day and a half, mind you, but somewhere along the line.'

'Would you?'

'I'm pretty sure.'

'How?'

'How else? By putting it to work where it would do a decent amount of good.'

'And where's that?'

Amy smiled. 'I'm too shy to tell you. But I've ego enough not to worry about getting it done.'

A knock at the door. Amy opened it to Margaret Duncannon.

During Margaret's visits to her sister, Helen had caught enough glimpses of her one time or another to know who she was. But obviously this was not reciprocal. There was a natural congeniality in Margaret's smile, but no recognition.

'Sorry,' she said. 'I thought . . . Is Wiley around?'

'Helen, this is my friend the boss's wife,' Amy said. 'Margaret, this is my friend the private cop.'

Amy meant to say more. It was clear she did, meant to go on and redress her flippancy with a sensible, full-scale set of introductions but she never got the chance. The change in Margaret's expression was astonishing. In seconds a sort of abstracted mildness became rage—hot-eyed and riveting.

'God, God, you—' But then her teeth came down hard on her lower lip. She spun around. It was as if only retreat could keep her from savagery.

Amy hurried to the door after her, and half way down the corridor Margaret did stop long enough to say, voice trembling, 'Tell Wiley for me I can't do Gertrude.'

'He'll be back in—'

'Please, Amy, *you* tell him.' Doors slamming, then silence.

Amy whistled. 'That's the most upset I've ever seen her,' she said. 'Hell, that's more upset than I ever thought she could be. What in God's name did you do to her?'

'Nothing.'

Amy glanced at Helen gaugingly.

'Nothing, I swear. I've never so much as spoken a word to her.'

'Or staked her out in the line of duty?'

'I'd remember.'

'You're sure?'

Helen nodded. 'My career isn't old enough yet so the cases have begun to blur.'

They stared at each other—witnesses to the sudden flash of a phenomenon. At length Helen got up. 'I'd better go,' she said. 'You were very kind to talk to me. I won't come back unless you ask me to. That's the way to do it, isn't it?'

'Yes.'

Helen hesitated. 'I can't leave without saying how much I've enjoyed watching you on the stage. Jacob, too. We're fans.'

'Thanks,' Amy said, but as if her mind were elsewhere. Her feet beat out a slow, contemplative kind of rat-a-tat-tat, and Helen thought she seemed a shade reluctant to turn loose. Helen had the feeling some final piece of communication might be on its way. But she was wrong.

'Yeah, thanks,' Amy said, smile brilliant now. 'Listen, you can stake me out any time.'

Margaret Duncannon was in the lobby, pacing. On seeing Helen she immediately crossed to her—and, outrageously, her right fist was cocked. Helen came to a dead stop but said nothing. She kept her eyes on Margaret's and her body alerted. Margaret did not swing after all. By force, as if her arm were solid lead, she drew it down. She dug into her handbag for a handkerchief.

'How could one woman behave so disgustingly to another?' Crying bitterly now.

'Really, I don't know what you're talking about. If you'd just calm down and—'

'Liar, liar!'

And then, as before, she was in desperate retreat.

Helen felt someone staring at her. It was the honey-blonde, saucer-eyed.

# CHAPTER 6

Jacob had interrogated Karen Duncannon the Monday after Ellie's murder and found her aggressively unco-operative. She had never really liked Jacob. Or Helen, for that matter. It might have been that she sensed instinctively where their sympathies would lie if it came to domestic trouble. At any rate, almost from the first, she had made it clear they were Neil's friends, not hers. And that if she fed them occasional meals, played occasional sets of tennis with them, it was merely a matter of *noblesse oblige. Her* class trained its females to do their duty.

But when she entered his office this time Jacob saw that something had changed. She was more subdued, less sure of herself. She seemed interested in the possibility of making a good impression. It wasn't precisely that she wanted to trade on an old relationship; no, that wasn't quite it, he thought. But at least she was disposed to acknowledge that one had existed. She asked after Helen, asked if he had heard from Neil, began, suddenly, a reminiscence in the middle of which she found herself cut off. Jacob had decided that if she were being amiable, it was probably worthwhile tactics for him not to be.

'Why don't you stop pulling my chain and just tell me?' he said.

Dots of colour. She braced quickly, however. 'Tell you what?'

'What I'll find out anyway. Not smart to withhold information from the police. People who do that complicate their lives.'

'You are a boor, Jacob. I wonder why I ever let myself forget that.'

She wore her dark, glossy hair tightly pulled back, exposing well-shaped ears. But it seemed to him that these had flattened to the sides of her skull like the ears of a horse when it listens hard and is afraid. And so, crossing his arms on his chest, he sat back to wait.

'May I at least have a cup of coffee?'

Boor-like, Jacob bellowed for his guardian sergeant, Herman Gordon, whose desk formed a buffer between Jacob and a world of potential Horowitz-molesters. Herman's large and rumpled form filled the doorway. Through the thick lenses of his bifocals, he inspected Karen invidiously, as if in fact she were not the handsome female she was generally conceded to be. He took her order and then lumbered away, muttering about what was and wasn't in his job description. This was not usually Herman's way. Something about Karen was inimical to him. Jacob guessed that something about Karen would be inimical to all large, rumpled men. (He included himself.) And the other way around, of course.

She wore a short khaki skirt that set off breathtaking legs and a navy blouse discreetly buttoned to the top but transparent enough to reveal fetching glimpses of underwear. Her clothes looked simple but expensive. The double row of pearls she played with looked expensive, too. She had a view of pearls, he remembered. 'No one should wear them who doesn't know how. I know how. I can wear them any time, anywhere.' He recalled that she had once worn them to the tennis court.

Herman returned. 'All out of milk again,' he said to Jacob, as if a language barrier existed between her species and his. 'Will she drink it black?'

'Yes, yes.' Impatiently, a dismissive wave of her hand.

He went, glowering.

'I've withheld nothing,' Karen said. 'What I'm about to tell you I didn't know the last time I saw you. Not that it's all that much anyway.'

Jacob kept silent.

'They had a quarrel.'

'Who did?'

'Alec and Margaret.' She hesitated. 'The night Ellie was murdered.' Her glance touched his, then slid away, conveying some meaning between fretful and fearful. Suddenly she sat up very straight. She spoke sharply. 'So what? I don't see how a quarrel between Alec and Margaret can possibly connect to Ellie's death. Do you?'

'What did they quarrel about?'

'Oh, what difference does that make? They quarrelled. They are husband and wife, so they quarrelled. I imagine that even in your idyllic marriage quarrels sometimes happen. And does it ever really make much difference what you quarrel about?'

'You say you didn't know about the quarrel until—when?'

'Yesterday.'

'How did you find out?'

'I found out, that's all.'

He bellowed for Herman again, asked for and got his notes covering their original interview. He consulted these. He looked at her hard. It seemed to him she was now rolling the pearls as if they were beads; that is, with religious fervour.

Quoting: '"My sister and her husband dined with me at my apartment. After that we watched TV until shortly after ten."' He glanced up. 'Is that the truth?'

'Of course it is.'

'When did the quarrel take place?'

She hesitated. 'Before they arrived,' she said finally.

'You seem uncertain.'

'It could have been before, it could have been after. A quarrel's a quarrel, isn't it, whenever it happens.'

Quoting again: '". . . we watched TV until shortly after ten.' Who's we?'

She kept silent.

He spoke reflectively. 'My, how I wish there was a way

to keep our jails clean. And then there's that god-awful stench . . .'

'Alec left right after dinner,' she said. 'Seven-thirtyish.'

'Because of the quarrel?'

'Yes.' Then, realizing how poorly this accorded with her previous uncertainty, she corrected herself. 'I mean no, of course.' She shook her head. 'What I mean is, how would *I* know? Damn you, Jacob Horowitz, if you want people to tell you the truth, you shouldn't hammer at them the way you do.'

'All right, I've stopped hammering,' he said. 'Take your time. Collect yourself and tell me the truth.'

She took a sip of the coffee, decided it was undrinkable, and told him so, banging the mug down on the desk hard enough so that some of its contents sloshed over.

Jacob rescued papers but said nothing.

A culminating roll of pearls and then she reached back and deftly unclasped them. She dropped them into her purse which she snapped shut as if the pearls and not Jacob were what she wished to punish. Glaring at him, she said, 'They quarrelled before they got to my apartment, they were still quarrelling when they got there, and yes, it's why Alec left early. I lied to you about it—that is, I kept it from you simply because I felt it was none of your business.'

'Now tell me what they quarrelled about.'

'About Neil, if you must know. Actually it's the only thing they *ever* quarrel about.' Her mouth set in a slash of displeasure familiar to Jacob. 'He's remarkable, your friend Neil. First he spoils his own marriage, now he's at work on his brother's.'

Jacob wondered what a dispassionate observer might have made of that particular view of marriage Duncannon-style. He knew what he made of it. And though he kept his face expressionless, he knew she knew what he made of it.

And surprisingly this had an effect. She looked away. 'I didn't mean that the way it sounded,' she said.

'Didn't you?'

'No. I . . .' Now she met his eyes directly. 'I love Neil,' she said. 'I would do a great deal for him; anything, really, if we exclude live with him. Believe it or not, that's true. And I'll tell you something else you may find hard to believe. Something *he* finds hard to believe. I love him more than he ever loved me, more than he ever could. And I think that's really what broke us up. You're a smart man, Jacob. At least that's what everybody says about you. Are you smart enough to know how that works?'

He kept silent, and they stared challenges at each other for a moment. And then she said, 'But unlike you and Helen and Alec and even Margaret, I was never blind to his faults.'

'No, just to his virtues.'

'I hate you, Jacob Horowitz. God, how smug and self-righteous you always are.'

'You said they quarrelled about Neil. What specifically?'

'The same old refrain. Alec wants him in the business. Margaret says let him alone, let him find his own way.' She shook her head. 'I adore my sister, but sometimes she can be obtuse. Leave Neil to find his own way, and he'll be a street person inside a year. Only Alec can redeem Neil. He's his one hope of solvency.'

'I thought we were talking about redemption.'

'That's what I said, redemption.'

'You said solvency.'

She stood up, eyes tracking the room as if one of Jacob's superiors might be lurking in a corner. 'How dare you treat me like some . . . I don't have to take this from you.'

'Sit.'

Their glances engaged, skirmished, and Karen lost this one, too. With something of a thump she sat down again.

Jacob continued to stare bleakly at her. 'All right, let's see if I'm getting this straight. You barged in here today—'

'Barged?'

'No appointment. No phone call. *Barged.* Because . . .'

'Because I didn't want you flaying me alive if you found out about the quarrel some other way. I know how you are, Jacob.'

'I see. It's self-concern that brought you here.'

'Of course.'

'So overriding you were perfectly willing to throw someone else to the wolves.'

'What are you talking about?'

'Come on now. Until two minutes ago Alec Duncannon had an airtight alibi. All three of you did. Now only two of you do. He's odd man out.'

'That's absurd. Why on earth would Alec Duncannon need an alibi?'

He studied her. 'You're lying again,' he said.

Colour reappeared in her cheeks. He knew that appalling ways to behave towards him were kaleidoscoping in her brain, making it a form of torture to sit perfectly still, her back aristocratically straight, her hands as properly clasped in her lap as they had been the moment before.

'You're in here blowing smokescreens,' he said. 'To hide what? Damned if I know. But I will soon, and when I do I'll burn your pretty bottom with it.'

She got up. 'I've had enough,' she said. 'I'm leaving, and don't you dare try to stop me.'

He didn't.

'That is one pissed-off woman,' Herman said, thoroughly delighted to make the observation. He regarded Jacob, profoundly admiring. 'Didn't think guys like us could do that to broads like her.'

'She puts her pants on one leg at a time,' Jacob said, and the two large, rumpled men grinned at each other as the meek might on the day they come into their estate.

Wiley Tait was discomfited—he'd been kept waiting longer than he thought was necessary. Longer, in fact, than Jacob had intended, due to Karen's visit. But not so discomfited—or annoyed or irritated—Jacob saw, that he couldn't keep it in check. Jacob wondered if that were due to the basic good nature he was reputed to possess, or some other, more interesting reason.

Lowering himself into the chair that had just been vacated, Wiley said, 'If Karen's not careful she'll wake up one day and find herself distinctly steatopygous.'

'Pardon?'

'Fat-assed.'

Jacob decided not to be amused. 'Mr Tait, why do I have the feeling I'm much more interested in seeing this murder solved than you are?'

An instant sobering. 'For God's sake, man, she was my wife.'

'But somewhat less loving than seemed true the last time we talked.'

Wiley appeared nonplussed for a moment, but then his face cleared. 'You mean the new will,' he said.

'Did that come as a shock to you, Mr Tait?'

'A shock? No.' He smiled ruefully. 'If you wanted to call it a disappointment I wouldn't argue, but not a shock. Ellie was . . .' He fixed on a point above Jacob's head. The candid eyes narrowed, the frank, friendly expression showed effort appealingly as he sought an adequate finish to his sentence.

'Unpredictable,' he said. 'One of the most unpredictable women who ever lived.'

'This is Judge Duncannon we're talking about?'

'You didn't know her personally, Lieutenant, did you? So all you really have to go on is the conventional wisdom. None of that's unfounded, you understand. I mean, there *was* the iron discipline. There *was* the idealism that made her such a tough fighter for her causes, but there was the other Ellie, too—what Neil once called the Borgia side of her. Ask him about it. He suffered from it as much as I did.

Maybe more.' He paused reflectively. 'Maybe more than any of us.'

'Are you saying to me Neil had more reason to want her dead than anyone else?'

Appalled, Wiley sat up straighter. It was hard to doubt the quality of his outrage. 'I thought he was your friend,' Wiley said.

Jacob kept silent.

'Ah, you're a game-player, aren't you? An improviser. If a line pops into your head you'll try it out, won't you? Maybe it'll make something happen.'

'I haven't heard your answer.'

'The new will. That's still what this is all about, right?'

Jacob kept silent.

'Neil didn't know there was one. If he didn't know it existed how could it be a motive for wanting to see her dead?'

'Did you know it existed?'

'No.'

'So I guess I could say you did have a motive.'

Again Wiley took a moment to work it out. 'To prevent a new will from ever being drawn?' he asked.

Jacob said nothing.

'I see,' Wiley said. 'Yes, I suppose that's so.'

'Not just a motive,' Jacob said, 'a prime motive. Two million after taxes. The woods aren't full of motives as prime as yours. So put yourself in my place, Mr Tait. Here I finally have a suspect with a world-class motive and an uncorroborated alibi. Man, you just have to expect me to take that seriously.'

Wiley stood up. 'Listen, is it all right if I go to the men's room?'

Jacob summoned Herman again. The outsize genie materialized, was instructed, peered at Wiley benignly, and led the way.

Jacob watched after them, thinking about Herman's eyes, thinking about cataracts diagnosed as manageable, hoping this would turn out to be the case, wondering what office life was likely to be without Herman who, after twenty-three years, was now a six-week span short of retirement. And then, once again, recalling that line about acting and the artful lie. If it took a thief to catch a thief, did it also take an actor to catch an actor? Self-pityingly, Jacob shook his head.

After which he forced himself to think constructively of Ellie Duncannon. Not easy either. As many views of her as there were Duncannon-watchers. And it wasn't that these were wildly diverse. On the contrary, they were so similar they fostered an illusion of tangibility. You could almost persuade yourself you had come to grips with her. Next thing you knew someone laid a nuance on you, and she was gone again, leaving behind damp hands and the faint, fishy smell of Slippery Eel.

A much more self-possessed Wiley returned and sat down. He glanced at Jacob's favourite photo of Helen framed in leather on his desk: black and white. Mornings, before the sun slivered through the blinds, she looked like a female shaman with forbidding things to say about the future. Later in the day the smile lines became apparent. Doom-struck Apache gave way to near hedonist—a woman eager for pleasure, alive to absurdity and with a world view that did not preclude the idea of redemption. Like photo, like Helen, Jacob thought.

'Met her this morning,' Wiley said. 'I could see her as Lady Macbeth some day if she's interested.'

Jacob kept his face expressionless.

Lifting strong chin, firming well-shaped mouth, Wiley got to work. 'Let me save us both some time,' he said briskly. 'Let me tell you what I make of the will, since that's really why you got me down here, right?'

'I'm listening,' Jacob said.

'We had this fight, Ellie and I. I asked her to lend—'

'Lend?'

'Give,' he acknowledged. 'I asked Ellie to give me a last dollop of money to finish up Second Space. I wanted to double the seating capacity. That's all it would need to be absolutely perfect. She had kittens.'

'Why?'

'She started screaming about how all I cared about was her money. All she meant to me was cash flow. And so on.'

'And yet you had taken money from her before.'

'Yes.'

'Often before?'

'Not really often. I don't want you thinking of me as some sort of leech . . . But all right, yes, I had taken money from her . . . often enough.'

'In fact, that was sort of the basis for your marriage, wasn't it, that she would supply the money, and you would supply . . .'

Wiley winced. 'Yes, that was the understanding,' he said.

'And so the screaming and carrying-on was out of left field, correct?'

'I suppose so, yes.'

'How do you explain it?'

'I already did. I told you she was the most unpredictable woman alive.'

'And it was right after this she changed her will?'

'My guess is she called old man Linderman as soon as she threw me out of her office. But it wasn't the first time she changed her will, you know. And the thing is she would have changed it again if she'd had the chance. You probably don't believe that, but she would have.'

Jacob decided it was time to fire for effect. He said, 'Did you make love to your wife that Friday night?'

Wiley stared at Jacob. 'Are you telling me somebody did? Made love to her, I mean. Not . . .'

Jacob nodded.

Wiley exhaled heavily. 'How do you know?'

Convincing, Jacob thought. Surprise, a tincture of disbelief, now add a soupçon of resigned acceptance. Damn actors anyway. A murder case with actors in it was a murder case for his enemies.

'Take it as given, Mr Tait,' Jacob said. 'You were not the lover in question?'

'You forget. I wasn't even in town.'

'I didn't forget.'

Wiley, however, was no longer seriously attentive—to Jacob. A lot of activity was going on behind those alerted brown eyes, but the focus was inward. Jacob wished he could share that focus.

The phone rang. When Jacob picked it up and heard the high-pitched hilarity he instantly identified Lawyer Linderman.

'Got something for you. Wasn't going to give it to you and then decided she might've wanted me to.'

'Who?'

'Ellie, you damn fool. Who else would I be talking about? Want it?'

'Yes, please.'

The cackle again. 'Then get over here; that is, if you want to know who killed Ellie. Better come quick before I change my mind.'

The connection was broken abruptly. Jacob told Wiley who the caller had been and what had been said. And watched with interest.

Not a flicker. 'Old men tend to self-dramatize,' Wiley said. 'After all, what could he have?'

Jacob thought he asked the question carefully.

'For a homicide cop guessing's bad form,' he said.

But ten minutes later, as he stepped into an elevator in the Tri-Town Attorneys' building, Jacob allowed himself to acknowledge the guess he'd instantly made. He'd guessed that what Lawyer Linderman had come upon among Judge Duncannon's relics was a Richard Grant tape. He acknowledged also how tremendously eager he was to have this in his hands. Ninety seconds after that, he guessed it wasn't going to happen.

Sybil Linderman remained ashen. By now, however, the office suite was cleared of all the official types that constituted the inevitable by-product of sudden death. Only the plump, blue-haired secretary, Miss MacPherson, sobbing quietly in a chair in the far corner of the room, and Jacob were left behind.

'Do you have a cigarette?' Miss Linderman asked.

'Don't smoke,' Jacob said.

'Neither do I. Nor do I want one. My God, I'm talking gibberish. Does anyone ever say anything intelligent at times like these?'

'I don't think it's mandatory,' Jacob said. 'Listen, is there someone you'd like me to call?'

'No.' She smiled thinly. 'I'll have to make do with you. Do you mind?'

She was seated at her father's desk. On it was a still life ready to be titled 'A Lawyer's Working Day'—several neatly labelled and arranged manila folders; two sheafs of varisized documents; a yellow pad, the top page of which was half filled with well-trained, though slightly shaky handwriting, and a thick, dark green volume, opened, that could only contain pertinent precedents or cases in point. Everything looked in reasonably good order, Jacob thought. Not the kind of disreputability a posthumous examination would some day turn up on his own desk. She lifted one of the folders. Jacob saw it had Judge Duncannon's name on it. She didn't notice that—or anything.

'He kept asking "Why? Why? Why?" You'd think at ninety-one he'd know why. Or at least know enough not to ask the question.' She bent over her arms, burying her face. 'God, I'm going to miss him.'

The dirge-like sobbing of the two women filled the room with ancient counterpoint. Jacob listened and thought about death—not the old man's, his own. He tried to imagine the world without him. He got nowhere with that. He narrowed it to the Tri-Towns. Even that proved unimaginable. He thought of Helen bereft. It filled him with such sadness that he knew if he continued to sit there his tears would swell the chorus. He got up and went to the window. The street was bathed in sunlight. Ant-like people followed purposeful paths to single-minded objectives. None of them cared that he was mortal, he thought resentfully.

Sybil Linderman took a deep breath. 'I'd have put my arms around you,' he said, turning, 'but I wasn't sure you'd like it.'

'Want to try it now?'

He did.

Miss MacPherson's woe continued uncomforted.

'What kind of tape were you looking for?' Miss Linderman asked, breaking away.

'Just a tape. You'll know it if it turns up.'

She looked at him. 'Big men are often very kind,' she said. 'I've noticed that before. It's as if their size has kept them from being buffeted too much, and so they don't run scared.'

They stood for awhile listening to the soft, steady sobbing coming unabated from the other side of the room. He said goodbye. He had almost reached the door when she stopped him.

'Wait. I did find something you might be interested in. I almost forgot. I was going to call you. Not a tape, but . . .' She reached into the folder with Judge Duncannon's name on it and brought out an envelope with Jacob's name on it. She gave it to him. He withdrew a smudged and wrinkled slip of paper. It was from a pink three-by-five telephone memo pad. He read:

'Theater in the Square. Sent: $840.50 cash. 8/13.'

'Her handwriting,' she said.

'Where did you find it?'

'Just generally among her things.'

'Mean much to you?'

'No. But I think it did to my father. He smiled when I showed it to him, that cat-canary smile he gets when he's a step ahead.' She was smiling, too. But it withered as she realized the tense was out of kilter. She shook her head, turning from him.

He waited.

When he turned back she said, 'He burned some papers—'

'Papers?'

'Must have been papers. If it had been a tape I would have smelled it. At any rate he burned something. Just after he called you. I think he would have burned the memo, too, if . . .' She broke off before the enormity represented by the words heart attack.

He examined the memo again. 'Looks as if she paid someone in cash. Sent someone some cash. Someone or something to do with Theater in the Square. Wiley?'

She kept silent.

'The date might be interesting,' he said.

'The day before the murder,' she said.

'On the other hand maybe it's not interesting at all. Maybe it's not even a date,' he added glumly. 'May I keep it?'

She nodded. He started out again, and again he stopped. He came back and handed her a card. She read it and looked at him.

'Helen Horowitz? Is she your wife?'

'Yes.'

'I'm puzzled.'

He shrugged, slightly embarrassed. 'She's . . . I just thought she might be useful to you.'

'For when I need a private investigator?'

'Hell, no,' he said, glaring. 'For when you need a friend.'

## CHAPTER 7

Helen had four phone calls that morning and a visitor. The first of the calls was a wrong number, the other three were generated by her Yellow Pages listing. Of these, one was a lonely old man eager to talk; another hung up on hearing her voice, saying that if he wanted a female snoop he'd hire his wife; and the third was a 'live one', Helen told herself. The live one wanted to know Helen's rates. When informed, she then asked if Helen could see her at half past three that afternoon. When assured the time was hers, she went suddenly silent, after which she screamed, 'My lover Lewis is cheating on me, I know he is.' And hung up. Helen decided she was greatly in need.

The visitor came bearing gardenias. He was Richard Grant. She seated him.

'You look surprised to see me,' he said.

'I am a little. But then I'd be surprised to see almost anyone.' She found a vase for the flowers and set it on the bookcase. She returned to the desk. 'Business will come, however. I refuse to think negatively.' She told him about Lewis's lover and her hopes for her.

'Cause for celebration,' he said. 'Come to lunch.'

She found herself reaching instinctively for a workable excuse.

'Thanks, but I've had my lunch,' she said. 'And believe it or not, I'm expecting a call.'

'An important call,' he amended, as if the adjective had

been dropped inadvertently, requiring him to catch the slippery thing and put it in place.

'Believe it or not,' she said.

'I don't believe it,' he said, 'but the message is getting through.'

'What message?'

He looked at her speculatively. 'Why do you think I'm here?'

'If it's for a particular reason, I have no idea.'

Eyebrows in sceptical v's. 'Now I doubt that,' he said. 'I very much do. In the event that it's true, however, I am probably about to shock you. But I don't mind. Nor should you. The occasional shock is beneficial. It opens one's pores.'

He paused as if gathering thoughts. Helen didn't believe they needed gathering. She construed them as constantly available, as grazing at the top of his mind: a glib, facile herd.

'I am a man who likes being in love,' he said.

'Is that the shocking part?'

'Not quite.'

He wore a double-breasted navy blazer, white shirt (for his tan), light blue tie (for his eyes), and cream-coloured tropical trousers. He didn't look much like a judge, Helen thought, but then that was equally true of three-quarters of the Tri-Towns bench, for worse reasons.

'As you might imagine,' he said, 'I think of myself as a connoisseur, and those I choose to fall in love with all have something in common. They are splendid representatives of their types. I say this to you for obvious reasons.'

'Because you've chosen to fall in love with me?'

'I have.'

'And is Amy Ashbogen a splendid representative of her type?'

'She was. Before she turned vulgar.'

'When did that happen?'

He smiled. 'Guess.'

'Around the time she . . . what? Switched allegiances?'

'Around that time, yes. Splendid people have tastes to

match. Now I'd be the last to argue Neil Duncannon isn't a pretty enough sort of boy in his own way, but you would hardly call him splendid, would you?'

'Probably not.'

A shrug, Gallic in nature, inviting her to agree the point had been made.

'Probably the list doesn't end with me, though, does it? I mean the Splendid Representative list.'

To her surprise this drew a flicker of annoyance. 'List? There is no list,' he said. 'You mustn't think of me as some sort of Dracula, gorging on lovers for the sake of survival. Which is to say indiscriminately. I *select*, my dear. Carefully. I might almost say painfully. I choose one at a time to share a season with me for our mutual benefit.'

'And the fact that I have a husband doesn't make me ineligible, right?'

'Clearly not.'

'Suppose I were to clue Jacob in.'

'You won't. You're not the kind. You're the kind who manages this sort of thing for herself, yea or nay.' Mock sigh. 'In my case nay, I gather. What a shame. We might have been wonderful together. And on the tennis court, I did think you were sending signals.'

'You were wrong.'

'I'm never wrong,' he said. 'You've had second thoughts, that's all. A failure of nerve. Well, I don't push, I don't force, but I shall remain at your service. That is, if you should find yourself thinking yet again.'

'I won't.'

He reached over and brushed the back of his hand against her cheek. It was as if, in the same motion, his fingernail had scratched *the* most vulnerable spot on her spinal column.

'Gather ye rosebuds,' he said.

She stood. 'I'd rather not.'

'Oh, come now, hostility? Why on earth should you be anything but flattered?'

'Sorry. Can't help myself. My flesh is beginning to crawl.'

He got up too, smile gone. Without it he looked much older; far less confident; no longer the sure-footed seducer; more the ageing Don Juan. Her rejection to cause all this? Such a small pebble for such a major ripple.

'If I were you,' he said, viperish now, 'I would certainly *not* tell my husband. He still has his way to make in this town, after all. And as a lot of people can tell you, I'm a bad enemy.'

He left. She made a dash for the closet, dug out the freshener Jacob had bought her on the theory that a certain share of her market would be cigar-smoking, and used it to good purpose.

## CHAPTER 8

Around 2.0 p.m. it began to rain, one of those relentless rains which seem not so much a caprice of the weather as a curtain let down by nature to separate seasons. Summer on its way to history. Jacob told Herman to pick him up in half an hour, then ran from the limo to the three-storey brownstone that harboured Alec Duncannon, Inc. Twenty paces, no more, but he was thoroughly wet. In his wake Herman yelled something centering on the word umbrella. Jacob turned. Herman was lumbering after him with that artefact clutched in his hand.

'Who are you, my mother?'

'Last summer you caught a cold and made us all miserable,' Herman said.

'Two summers ago.'

'Whatever.'

'Who'll wipe my nose after you've gone?'

'I've left instructions.'

He took on puddles like a dancing bear. Jacob, watching, grinned.

A few minutes later he was following a lissome young secretary—Miss MacPherson's antithesis—into the office of the agency's CEO, who was not glad to see him. But then he hadn't been glad to see Jacob the first time around. In Jacob's view Alec Duncannon had the kind of core dourness that suggested he was not often glad to see anyone. And yet, according to Neil, there were those two great exceptions: Neil himself and Margaret. Sceptically, Jacob internalized a general order to wait and see.

Alec was on the phone, fingers drumming, toes tapping, losing patience. Finally he said, 'All right, damn it, I'm coming out.' As plastic hit plastic a small wedge broke off, and Jacob wondered how many phones per year failed to survive.

'You sure know how to pick your days,' Alec said to Jacob and shot by him.

Alone, Jacob's attention was caught by the Margaret gallery. He crossed the room for a closer look. Beautiful child, beautiful woman, he thought. She had that rare thing: true sweetness. And qualities related to it. Openness, for instance. You could almost say defencelessness. As he moved from photo to photo he was struck by this. It was as if, so certain was she of the world's tenderness towards her, she had never found it necessary to develop a shell. Helen had told him about the strange encounter at the theatre. What could have caused such a reaction? Mistaken identity? No other explanation came readily to mind. He examined a picture of Margaret in summer whites—T-shirt, shorts, sneakers—a brown, floppy-eared pooch in her lap. Both had spaniel eyes, he thought. Who would willingly bring anxiety to either face?

He shifted to the Neil corner, grinning to see his friend as a ten-year-old. The pose, borrowed from some movie, was pugnacious. Left leg forward, left shoulder lowered, right hand cocked to take out a bad guy. A juvenile Cagney or Bogie. Jacob's grin faded. What *about* Neil? *Did* the revised will make him a suspect? Helen believed wholeheartedly in the concept of money and Neil as antipathetic. If she was right, it separated him from much of his species. If she was wrong . . . Where the hell *was* Neil anyway? Exiled by Ashbogen decree? OK. But did that mean he had to fall off the face of the earth?

Alec returned, still fuming. He saw where Jacob was positioned and raised his own question. 'Have you heard from him?'

'I was hoping you might have,' Jacob said.

'Me? I'm only his brother.'

He moved to his desk. One of the bottom drawers was open, and he kicked at it, soccer-style, catching the edge with his shin. Jacob was sure it hurt, but if that were so the pain nerves never got the message to his face.

'Life,' Alec said. 'What's the best thing about it?'

Jacob was not willing to commit himself.

'It's short,' Alec said.

'I guess that means your sister's got it made now,' Jacob said experimentally.

'She always had it made. She always had it exactly the way she wanted it. She played the tune, the rest of us danced.'

'Even her murderer?'

'If you think that's impossible it's because you never knew her.'

Jacob thought about ambiguity and how frequently Ellie's friends and relatives connected it to her. It was as if being fooled, puzzled, and even hurt by her had become, in a curious way, a matter of pride. Like the Purple Heart, a badge of honour earned for a wound.

'I wonder why she changed her will,' he said.

'Why? I'll tell you why. To get at me . . . that is, to get Neil away from me. Without her money in his pocket I had some control over him. Not a lot, but some. Now . . .' He got up and went to the window. 'God, I hated that bitch.'

Jacob kept his face expressionless.

Alec turned, his face equally so. 'Enough to kill her? That's what you need to know, right?'

'I guess.'

'The only one I hate that much is . . .' He took a deep breath and returned to his desk. 'Sorry,' he said. 'What the hell, none of this is your fault.'

The phone rang. He picked it up and listened for a moment like an ancient Roman trying for stoicism while Visigoths swarmed in the streets. 'Tell Henderson to call me,' he said and put down the phone. For a moment he was silent. The moment ended explosively, and he was on his feet again, pacing. 'Leaves us sucking hind tit this way. He ought to be—' He broke off, aiming a gun-like finger at Jacob. 'Roger Henderson's an account supervisor of mine. In my mind's eye I see him clutching his chest where the big pain is. In the next minute he'll gasp, his knees will buckle, and he'll pitch forward on his face. He owes all that to Neil, to the campaign Neil didn't develop, to the non-existent campaign client committed two million dollars to this very morning. Are you with me? There's no Neil, so there's no campaign.'

'No one can fill in for him?'

Alec stared, then snarled. 'Goddam amateur. You think there's nothing to this business, don't you? You think any smart-ass can be a copywriter. It's all jingles and clever puns and . . . What you can't connect to is that Neil is a natural. He does stuff only a handful can do. Everybody thinks I want him to stay here because . . . who the hell knows what they think? The truth is I want him here because he's great, because he's got a God-given talent for doing work that breaks through the clutter, ads that are just so goddam marvellous people are compelled by them. And I mean people who hate advertising. And I don't think he's got the right to turn his back on a talent like that.' The anger seeped out of him, and now there was something imploring in his expression. 'Is that so hard to understand?'

'No,' Jacob said.

Once more the phone clamoured for attention. Alec responded without haste, fingers and toes still, voice well modulated, a man in control of his emotions. 'Yes, Roger.' Pause for listening. It took only a moment for his face to become scarlet. 'Damn you, I *was* out there. I *did* look at those layouts. What do I think? I think they're ordinary. I think they're banal. I think you'll spend thirty grand for photography, and when you're through you'll have a dog's breakfast of a campaign because there's no idea behind it.' And yet again phone met cradle with bruising impact. He picked it up at once and roared, 'No calls.' After which he turned to Jacob. 'You got something to say to me, say it.'

'I think it's the other way around,' Jacob said.

'Listen, no games. I'm in no—'

Jacob held up his hand. 'I don't want to hear that, Mr Duncannon. I want to hear why you lied to me.'

Alec looked up at the ceiling, where he saw either a costly series of cracks or the outline of a troublesome future. Because when he turned to Jacob again his face was bleak.

'The goddam doorman,' he said.

Jacob kept silent.

Alec smiled, the mouth-thinning, mirthless kind. 'Oh, what a tangled web we weave. Right?'

'Where did you go after you left Karen's?'

'He had his back to me, bullshitting with that big-tit broad on the security desk, and I thought I'd made it by him. I should have known better. I should have recognized the type—pure son of a bitch with eyes in the back of his head for every scam coming down the pike. I hope he croaks.'

'I'm waiting,' Jacob said.

'So wait. Until hell freezes over.'

Jacob sensed that once again—as so often before in this

case—truth was wearing dark glasses. But he saw also that a decision had been reached: clam up. Still, he decided to take a last shot.

'If you were seen coming out of the apartment building,' he said, 'maybe you were seen going into the theatre.'

'That would've been amazing,' Alec said, 'since I wasn't anywhere near the theatre.'

His eyes met Jacob's unflinchingly. After a moment he elaborated. Things on his mind, he'd just walked around until tired enough to sleep. No, he didn't know how long he'd walked. No, no one saw him. No, he didn't give a goddam whether Jacob believed him or not. That last was tacit but communicated none the less.

Finally the two men just sat there looking at each other, both big-chested, both with heavy arms crossed over these chests. It's doubtful either had enough detachment at that moment to realize how much they resembled book ends. It was as if they both had grown chess-weary at precisely the same time and now, spent and morose, could only wait for their energy levels to climb again, restoring, respectively, their competitive edges.

'I feel old,' Alec said suddenly. 'You ever have days when you feel like that?'

'Yeah,' Jacob said.

Alec studied him. 'Today?'

'Either that, or I'm catching cold.'

'You know when you know you're old?'

'When?'

'When you stop worrying so much about death. When it scares you a lot less because you're readier for it. I mean, I don't think getting old has all that much to do with chronology. Yeah, sure, that sounds stupid and trite, but it's true. When you begin to see the bright side of death, it's because you've gone and grown old. Old as the hills.'

'You think that's the point your sister might have reached?'

Alec had been focused elsewhere. This brought him back. 'Ellie? What's she got to do with this?'

'Maybe you've been saying someone did her a favour?'

'Someone like me?'

Jacob kept silent.

Alec held out his hands. '*Mea culpa*. What happens now? You read me my rights and I call my lawyer?'

Jacob got to his feet and left, forgetting his umbrella.

Back at the precinct, he stopped at Herman's desk for messages.

'Guy waiting for you in your office,' Herman said.

'Who?'

'Says his name's Hummel, doorman at the Lancaster Arms.'

He was red-haired with boozer's eyes and wrestler's heft, and he grinned arrogantly as Jacob opened the door. He was sprawled in a chair, one foot braced against Jacob's desk. He was truly large, even larger than Jacob to whom it seemed—after Wiley and Alec, to say nothing of Herman and himself—that in the past hour the national average had taken a thirty-pound spurt. He kicked the man's foot away from his desk as he went by. He considered it a point of honour to have done so.

'What the hell's wrong with you?'

The man had half risen from the chair, but Jacob's finger directed him back again. He hung fire for a moment, but then obeyed. He looked a shade less confident.

'Came here of my own free will,' he said, as if he'd memorized a speech.

Jacob waited.

'Got some information. Valuable information. You don't want it say so, and out I go. Who gives a shit.'

'What is it?'

The bloodshot eyes turned crafty. 'Not without immunity.'

Jacob sighed, stood, came over to the other side of the desk, grabbed handfuls of shirt, dragged his visitor to the wall and slammed him against it. It was heavy work, but he enjoyed it.

Twenty minutes later, good humour quite restored, Jacob knew for sure the why of Karen Duncannon's surprise visit.

## CHAPTER 9

After bellowing her name to no avail, Jacob finally discovered his wife at her ease under a tub-full of bubble bath, a martini in one hand, a left-over turkey leg in the other—Helen the Eighth.

'There's one for you in the fridge,' she said. 'Martini, that is. No more turkey legs. Not to worry. We're celebrating at the Hornpipe. Half past seven.'

He headed for the refrigerator. When he returned he delved into the matter of the celebration. In explanation, she detailed the visit of Ann Margaret Hardesty, age fifty-five, whose fury concerning the inconstancy of Louis de Paolo, age sixty-two, had resulted in a three-day assignment at a hundred and fifty dollars a day plus expenses.

'Actually, I only dared ask a hundred. I told her a hundred over the phone, but when she came in she insisted on the extra fifty. With Ann Margaret Hardesty, it's axiomatic you get what you pay for. Who needs a cheapie detective, she said. You'd like her, Jacob. Skinny, but feisty, and very up front. Her husband made a small fortune as a beer distributor, and I gather she's done a good job of holding on to it. In other words she's foolish about Louis but damn little else. My charge is to find Louis with his sweetie and provide Mrs Hardesty with the evidence, which she'll use as she sees fit. Probably to drive him bananas. *Is* there a sweetie? Mrs Hardesty says until two months ago he was a bull in bed. Since then he's turned definitely bearish.'

'Maybe he crested. Sixty-two isn't thirty.'

'Maybe.'

'You think there is a sweetie?'

'I think Louis's a rat; a rat-fink fancy man, is what I think. I'll show you his picture. A shark, a leech, exploiting rich widows like Mrs Hardesty all over the country. Stop grinning at me.'

'It's a cause?'

'Where's the harm if it is?'

He thought there might be harm but didn't feel much like raining on parades just then, so he changed the subject. After patting his pockets a moment or two he found Ellie Duncannon's memo. He gave it to her. She read it, then looked up questioningly.

'On August thirteenth Wiley Tait was sent money for Theater in the Square purposes,' he said. 'That's the message, right?'

She read it aloud: 'Theater in the Square. Sent: $840.50. Cash. 8/13.' She nodded. 'Seems likely.'

'I just had another thought, thanks to Mrs Hardesty.'

'My Mrs Hardesty?'

He took a sip from the martini, peered into the glass as if for portents, then placed it blindly—that is, precariously—on the rim of the tub. Helen moved it to the floor.

'For $64,000, name your two largest competitors.'

'The local branch of Pinkerton's and Sentinel, Inc.'

'Sent. Sentinel,' he said.

Her eyes lighted. They then discussed Buck Foley, a former police officer, a friend, and, as events proved, an accomplished entrepreneur. In five years he had converted Sentinel, Inc. from an extra name on his apartment mail box to the formidable local rival of investigative giants. Buck was Helen's inspiration. In turn, he was fond enough of her to have offered employment, and when that was declined, vital how-to-do-it counsel.

'So what I'm holding here is a memo covering a transaction between Ellie Duncannon and Sentinel, Inc.? For what purpose?' she asked.

'That's where Mrs Hardesty comes in.'

'How? Wait a minute, wait a minute. You're telling me Ellie Duncannon suspected Wiley Tait of . . . with whom, for heaven's sake?'

'Don't know. Anyway I'm not telling, I'm guessing. Sent could mean sent.'

'Want me to call Buck?'

He thought about it. 'Let it go till tomorrow. I don't think I could handle it just now if it came up snake-eyes.'

She surveyed him diagnostically. After a moment she said, 'You're catching cold, Jacob, I can tell. It always gets you in your self-confidence.'

The Hornpipe was a pricey restaurant they liked and reserved for special occasions. It had two floors, solid oak tables, red and white checked cloths, nautical flotsam and jetsam clinging like barnacles to its panelled walls, and wide windows through which you could watch the bay shine and shimmer now that the rain had ended. They ordered champagne. They ate and drank with maximum gusto and minimum conversation until the lobster was skeletal and the split history.

It was the silence of repletion. Finally Helen said, 'Well, I've seen Neil's lady-love. Now I guess we better check out his house. On our way home, OK?'

'OK,' he said, pretending the slight emphasis on we was an accident of phrasing and not a sealant on domestic division, which it certainly was. Having done the generous and appeasing thing, she now fixed a glance on him of particular import. It meant—and he knew it—that no precedent had been set.

He found fairly clean Kleenex in his pocket and blew his nose. 'Have you heard from him?' he asked.

'I have not.'

'If you had, would I know it?'

'Probably. Do we have to take this up now?'

'No.'

'Not on a celebration night, Jacob.'

'Right you are.'

They watched the bay. Helen saw a meteor slip glossily between two mermaids gambolling out near the pier. She sighed. 'I *have* been thinking about it,' she said. 'I mean this whole business of confidentiality. You're a cop, you know.'

'And a husband.'

'And a lover,' she said, patting his hand reassuringly. 'And my best and most trusted friend. And the soul of tact and discretion. And the answer is, if it seems right and proper and professional to me, yes, I will keep things from you.'

He was silent.

'Jacob, how could it be any other way?'

He was silent.

'Just as in the past you have kept things from me,' she said.

'Name once.'

She looked at him.

'Name five times,' he said.

'I could, you know.'

He was silent.

'*You* haven't thought about all this before?' she asked.

'Yes, but not hard. Flicked at it, hoping it would go away.' He paused. 'It could cause trouble,' he said.

'Not real trouble. Jacob, if I thought that I'd pack it in. Find something else to do. I mean it. Squabbles, that's different. We can handle those. We have them all the time.'

He grinned, then sneezed.

She dug a fat supply of gleamingly white Kleenex out of her purse and gave it to him.

The waiter came by to inveigle them into dessert, which they resisted, and as reward for this unwonted asceticism allowed themselves Irish coffee. They sipped, made appreciative noises. It was when Jacob began attracting attention that Helen decided to distract him.

She said, 'What I don't understand is why Schimmel . . .'

'Hummel.'

'Hummel reads in the paper that Alec Duncannon was at his sister-in-law's until after ten. OK, he knows better since with his own eyes he'd seen him leave sevenish. So he figures he can shake someone down about that. He tries it out on Karen. But when she says no deal, why does he come to you and risk a possible extortion rap?'

'Don't know,' Jacob said.

'Bull. You know everything.'

'All right, I'll take a guess. I'd guess he's one of the vengeance-seekers, our Mr Hummel; one of God's angry men. He'd rather visit the slammer than not get even.' She looked sceptical, so he added, 'My Aunt Daisy buried my Uncle Arthur in the clothes he died in because he had a massive heart attack on the tennis court, and she'd warned him not to play that day.'

'Yes,' she said, persuaded now. 'Milly Burgess. She threw my best blue strapless into Payote Lake after the Pædiatric Nurses' Senior Dance. She thought I took a man away from her.'

'What man?'

'So, are you going to bust Mr Hummel?'

Sneezing. Kleenexing. After which he decided he didn't really want to know what man—such knowledge never made him feel better—and answered *her* question.

'Karen won't press charges. She says the less she has to do with him the better. Probably, she would have paid him off. What stopped her, I think, is guessing it wouldn't end with once. She was right about that, of course. So all I could do really was tell Hummel I'd personally break every bone in his body if he didn't get out of town, and then have Herman drive him to the Connecticut border.' He paused. 'Maybe I should have had Herman follow him. Maybe he'd have led us to Neil.'

She stared at him. 'Joke?'

'How do I know what's a joke and what isn't? I sure as hell wish something would lead me to him. Why? You ask me why? How about M is for Motive?'

'That's ridiculous.'

'Because Neil hates money. I know. I'd like to talk to him anyway. For starters, about where he was that Friday night.'

'You know where he was—with Amy.'

'So she says.'

'You think she's lying?'

'In this case everybody lies. It's obligatory. And the fact is, she's in love with him. Women in love . . .' He paused, experienced a sense of floundering, and bulwarked himself classically. 'Ask D. H. Lawrence.'

She studied him. Then she shook her head. 'But isn't the point simply this, that Neil can't be a suspect? I mean, he truly can't be. Think about it, Jacob.'

Inwardly Jacob groaned. It was something that had been in mind since the day the case was first briefed to him. In his mind, yes, though shunted off to an out of the way corner, tailor-made for neglect. The unyielding core of it was that Ellie Duncannon had been screwed, *then* murdered.

'OK, who?' he asked.

'Who what?'

'Who'd she do it with? Was it someone we know? Was it someone *she* knew? Her husband? Who? Why are you looking at me that way?'

'I guess I have a hat to throw in the ring,' she said.

When she finished telling him about Richard Grant she

touched his hand. 'Jacob,' she said, 'nothing could be less important to me.'

He blew his nose and called for the check. 'Yeah,' he said. 'But one way or another . . . maybe not today, maybe not tomorrow . . . I'm going to have to cut his unimportant balls off.'

Having arrived at the door of the shapely white Colonial that neighboured theirs, Helen unlocked it. Mail was all over the place. The house felt empty, but otherwise it was unmarred. No dark and dreary birds flapping about in the attic. No sign that human intruders had defiled or damaged.

Coming back down the stairs, Helen saw the Linderman & Linderman envelope, peeking out from under several rolled-up copies of *Variety*. She rescued it. Clearly, it contained enclosures. She looked at Jacob, who watched impassively. She tore the envelope open. Inside was another envelope, sealed, Neil's name typed on it. She tore this open, too. Among the dozen photographs, eight were of reasonable quality. She recognized the colourful bedspread. She also recognized the two principals, though she had never seen them naked before: Wiley Tait and Margaret Duncannon. From photo to photo their range of expressions ran a gamut between surprise and fury. She didn't think they were acting. After flipping through, she handed the collection to Jacob.

'There seems to be a note,' Helen said. Withdrawing it, she unfolded and read it aloud:

> I forgive you. If I know you, Neil—and I do—you're shrugging boyishly and asking what for. Well, I *do* forgive you—for bringing him to me, your traitorous best friend. You're my brother, so I have no choice. But him? Never. When you read this, he'll be dead. I wanted to be sure you knew why.

Jacob took the note from her. No salutation, no signature. 'Looks like the same writing on the memo,' he said.

'Yes.'

They were silent a moment. Then Jacob said, 'But Wiley's not dead, is he? She planned to kill him but changed her mind? Is that what happened?'

'Or the plan missed fire.'

He nodded. He examined the postmark. 'Mailed three days ago, the day before Linderman died.'

'It was sitting around their office? The old man forgot about it until then?'

'Maybe,' Jacob said. 'I mean, that's certainly possible, but it could be Ellie gave him a sealed envelope with instructions to let fly on such and such a date.'

'Or a combination of both,' Helen said. She took the note from him, then handed it back. 'Look at the thickness of those t's. An angry, angry woman.'

'Yeah.'

'Now I can guess what had Margaret Duncannon half hysterical the day she met me. Amy introduced me as a private detective. Margaret must have decided on the spot I was connected to the picture-taking. Bulbs flashing, stuff going on like crazy. Maybe she never actually saw who did what.'

He nodded, watching her.

'I suppose Ellie suspected them for some time,' she said.

'Probably.'

She kicked the piles of mail. A copy of *Newsweek* struck the fireplace screen just right and toppled it, dislodging assorted pokers. The clatter was substantial and prolonged. 'I seem to be an angry woman, too,' she said.

'Why?'

'How would *I* know? Maybe it's because she looks so . . . incorruptible, so innocent. Like the last one in the world who'd ever mess around. If you were her husband you'd feel safe, wouldn't you? Oh, God, do you think Alec Duncannon knows? I'll bet he does. I'll bet Ellie told him, *showed* him. Think how lost he must be feeling, Jacob. He must have had such faith . . .'

Suddenly she moved into him, and, as if needing his bulk to block out the world, buried her face in his chest.

'She's just a person,' he said into her hair. 'Things happen.'

'I don't *want* things to happen.'

He thought about what he might say to that and almost spoke. But he didn't. He just held her until she was quiet.

She moved away. Locating her handbag, she dug out her compact, inspected her face, snarled at the ravages and repaired them. 'Back to business,' she said. When he reached a hand out to her, she returned it firmly. She took the envelope from him, hefting it to appraise its weight.

'You're thinking a set of photos might be what Linderman called you about?' she asked.

'An extra set maybe. And when he found it among Duncannon's things, maybe he decided he'd also found her killer. Understandable leap. Based on tried and true homicidal staples: infidelity, jealousy. Wives and husbands erase each other every day in a context like that. All right, now he'd identified the killer. Next step—turn him over and let the law take its course.'

With her toe she dug a delicate little ventilation shaft amid food market circulars. 'And then he had second thoughts?'

'He was ninety and cantankerous,' Jacob said. 'Maybe after calling me he suddenly decided he didn't want the law taking its course. So he burns the photos, thinking maybe it was the only set. He burns the photos to protect a guilty man, the ultimate cantankerous act.'

'Why? Why? Why?' Helen said, honouring the dead. 'Questions, questions, questions.'

'And answers. Lawyer Linderman took a supply of both with him.'

Helen went to the screen and righted it. She collected the

scattered pokers and restored them: pokers now decorously on parade. She did some other light housekeeping and then returned to Jacob's side.

'This house misses Neil,' she announced after a moment. 'And so do I.' She led Jacob out.

It was about 2.0 a.m. when Jacob awoke. 'Why? Why? Why?' he said, poking at Helen.

'What?'

'Homonymous, by God!'

She stared at him, worried.

'Not questions, baby. Not that at all. But maybe a dying man's attempt at sending a message.'

'What message?'

'Guess.'

'I can't. Tell me.'

'Isn't it out of character for that tough old buzzard to have died asking eternal questions? Sure it is. It bothered his daughter, and it's been bothering me. All right, but suppose after burning the photos he changed his mind *again*?'

'Would those be second thoughts? Or third thoughts? I've lost count.'

'What it would be is Lawyer Linderman struggling to say the name of a murderer.'

She stared at him, unenlightened.

'Do it yourself. What happens when you try three times to say Wiley and run short of breath each time?'

'Wi . . . Wi . . . Wi . . .' She grinned at him. 'You're marvellous,' she said.

'I have my good days,' he said modestly.

'Wi . . . Wi . . . Wi . . .' She repeated it once more, delighting in it. Her grin remained intact a long time before it lost substance and finally faded. She patted his hand in sympathy. 'Only one difficulty.'

He pretended not to hear.

'Jacob . . .?'

'Who do *you* think murdered Ellie Duncannon?'

'I don't know.'

'But you wouldn't bet the house on Wiley Tait, would you?'

He refused to answer.

## CHAPTER 10

Sal Crowley saw him coming and wheeled his chair forward. Peremptorily, he motioned Jacob to bend. Jacob did, and got his cheeks kissed. Somewhere between Marwood Place, their old neighbourhood, and the University of Pennsylvania's Wharton School, where he earned his MBA, Sal had adopted a continental manner. It was part Italian, part French, part Irish and often enough pure ersatz. By now, however, the manner had become the man, and Jacob, for one, thought Sal would be diminished without it. Every so often Sal made a pilgrimage to one of those old countries to get his manner shined up. He had recently returned from just such a journey, and the manner glistened and gleamed in the morning sunlight.

Jacob could think of fifty reasons for never wanting to set eyes on Salvatore Crowley, all having to do with the ways he earned his living (Sal was a Family man; not the very highest echelon in his market area, but high enough) and only one reason to be glad to see him, which was that he liked him.

He had always liked him. When they were boys on Marwood Place, Jacob had even then disapproved of Sal, whose path the Family had early marked. Through the years he had adopted various devices aimed at subverting the relationship. It was, after all, unsuitable. None had been successful. Jacob blamed his sense of humour. Inexplicably, it was so similar to Sal's that it produced a bonding. That having been said, however, the relationship was also defined by its limitations. Both were, in their own fashion, businessmen, and if it came to a showdown, business would be business. It was when he finally understood this that Jacob began to relax.

Sal, impeccable in brown bush jacket, yellow cravat, and white trousers, wheeled himself back to his lavishly stocked poolside bar to mix a martini the way he knew Jacob liked it. His upper torso was an athlete's, impressive even through his clothes. His lower half was useless, had been since a pipe bomb had exploded in his father's Maserati, Sal sitting next to him. The Family giveth and the Family taketh away. Dennis Crowley, Sal's father, had convinced someone powerful that he was overly ambitious. And thus, with Angelina Carlucci Crowley already dead, Sal had become an orphan and a cripple in the same instant.

'A sight for sore eyes, Jacob,' Sal said. 'Throughout all Europe I saw no sight as welcome as you. How is your Helen?'

'Good.'

'She is a shamus now, I hear.'

'You hear everything, Sal. You always did.'

He smiled. 'True. Even in the old neighbourhood, my intelligence was always best.'

Behind him, unsmiling, was Beauty Breit, Sal's chief of protocol. Jacob was surprised to see him there. There had been a rupture between Beauty and Sal, severe enough, Jacob would have thought, to preclude patching. Jacob, who had been witness to it, would have predicted either deep trouble of a lasting nature or very brief trouble indeed for Beauty. He'd been wrong. Beauty, in white bikini swimming trunks, was clearly still able to flex extraordinary muscles. He flexed them now provocatively, as an affront to Jacob, of whom he was not fond.

'Kilkenny cats, you and Beauty. Right, Jacob?'

It was the most blatant of rhetorical questions, and Jacob kept silent.

Sal motioned to the Olympic-sized swimming pool that covered most of the top floor of his Tri-Towns manor house and said, 'Cool off, young Tarzan. Jacob wishes to speak to me privately.'

Beauty narrowed chocolate brown eyes, but made no other protest. He pulled a sea-green cap over burnt gold curls and climbed to the diving-board. He plunged, his jack-knife a triumph of grace and power.

Sal applauded.

Beauty did a picture-perfect crawl, which Sal applauded too, in part to tease Jacob. He said, 'You are surprised to see him here?'

'I'm surprised to see him alive.'

'Well, I did intend to dispose of him, but then I realized how much I'd miss him. Who fetches and carries half so well? No one. Irreplaceable, my Beauty is.'

'Does he understand that enough to be grateful?'

'Beauty? Beauty understands everything that pertains to him. And nothing that pertains to anyone else. Now what can I do for you, Jacob?'

'Richard Grant,' he said.

Sal raised an eyebrow. 'A homicide cop sniffs around about the next governor of the state?'

'Is he your candidate?'

Sal studied him for a moment. Then he called to Beauty to come and join them. Beauty did, preening a bit before covering his splendid self with a blue silk wrapper.

'Beauty, Lieutenant Horowitz wants to know if Judge Grant is my candidate. What should I tell him?'

'To go—'

Sal cut him off. 'My friends are my friends,' he said. 'In this house they are treated with respect.'

'My friends are my friends, too,' Beauty said sullenly.

Sal stared hard, but Jacob sensed suddenly that he wasn't

quite as glossy as at first glance he had seemed. Here and there the shifting light picked up a worn patch. If this had been another time, an earlier time, Jacob thought, payment for insolence would have been instant. Beauty's nose might have been bleeding a river, or he might have found himself minus the lobe of an ear, and in neither case would Beauty have been surprised. Smarting certainly, but appeased in the way culprits always are when the punishment fits the crime. But that was then. Now Sal's stare softened and he said, 'A point worth making. Judge Grant is Beauty's friend. Whoever he belongs to as a candidate, he belongs to Beauty as a friend. *Claro*, Jacob?'

Jacob kept silent.

Beauty started towards the wheelchair ramp that led down into the house.

'Where are you going?' Sal called after him sharply.

'To see about lunch,' Beauty said over his shoulder but without stopping.

'Make it for three,' Sal said.

Beauty didn't answer.

Sal watched him. When he turned to Jacob his eyes were melancholy, and Jacob thought he could see signs of ageing. The tan, which he was never without, suddenly seemed brushed on rather than natural, and because of this, irrelevant. Not the deep tan, but the deep lines at both corners of his mouth commanded attention now. All at once pity for Sal was less gratuitous than it had been.

'As you can see,' he said, 'the status quo has shifted a bit. Things can be done about that. Should I do them, Jacob?'

But Sal's weary shrug made it clear that whatever those things were they remained more theoretical than operational. Also, despite the question, he seemed to have forgotten Jacob's presence.

'Grant,' Jacob said to remind him.

'Yes,' Sal said, reacting to the name. 'Judge Richard Grant, friend to Beauty. And to others as well.'

'What others?'

'You would know them.'

'Then he is connected. How high?'

'You would be impressed.'

'Your Uncle Angelo?'

'Since when is politics your business, Jacob?'

'Somebody knocked off Judge Duncannon. And if politics is at the root of that, then it's no longer just politics.'

'Politics is not at the root of it.'

Jacob kept silent.

'My word isn't good enough for you?'

Jacob gave serious thought to that and said no. And then added, 'No one's would be. Yours comes close. But I want more than your word, Sal.'

'What you want and what I decide to give could be two greatly different things.'

A momentary return to form. Jacob crossed his arms on his chest. His guess was he could wait it out. He was right.

Sal said, 'We knew Duncannon wore the FBI's wire, and at first were concerned, but only at first.'

'You knew? How?'

'We knew, we knew,' Sal said, irritated. 'Who the hell are you, Jacob—my father? My mother?—that I should reveal every goddam secret I ever owned? We knew, that's all. But with a wire, what matters of course is what it picks up. And what a wire picks up is *nada* if the party of the first part is minimally discreet. Judge Grant was warned to be discreet. Judge Grant knows well how to be discreet. He was born discreet and will die discreet. So, of what use would it be to us to waste Judge Duncannon? Do we welcome the speculations of idiot editorialists? Do we need visits from big bulls like Jacob Horowitz, shaking hell out of our delicate china? Answer!'

'All right,' Jacob said.

'Damn right, all right. And Jacob . . .'

'What?'

Admonishing finger. 'Be prudent. Money and muscle are united behind this switch-hitter Grant. My colleagues are ambitious for him. Are you listening to me? Stay out of their way.'

'Good advice, Sal.'

He sighed. 'And you'll take it if it's convenient. Ironhead, I have no more to say on the matter. Come inside. I will give you lunch while you still can eat it.'

Sal wheeled the chair to the ramp, and Jacob tagged after it. On and down. The pace was brisk, but Beauty was ready for him. As the chair reached bottom he caught it deftly with one hand and lifted Sal free with the other—an act of perfect timing and considerable strength. He eased Sal on to a sofa, covering his wasted legs with a brilliantly coloured, very expensive-looking shawl.

Sal's whole study was expensive-looking: handsome books with excellent titles, fine prints, deep leather furniture, walnut panelling, and the pervasive aura of civilized self-indulgence. It was a rich man's room, a cultured rich man's room. Both descriptions fitted Sal snugly enough without reference to any others that might also apply.

In a far corner a table was set for three. Jacob walked past it to the door, stopping when Sal called his name in protest.

'Jacob, poached salmon à la Crowley in your honour.'

'Can't.'

'A bottle of my best Chablis.'

'I'm in a hurry, Sal, but thanks. Some other time.'

'Beauty, it's because of you. He thinks you don't want him here. Urge him to stay.'

Beauty kept silent.

Jacob waved and exited. He heard footsteps tracking him but didn't slow. As he reached the front door, however, Beauty swung in front of him.

Beauty said, 'Things are different now. I wanted to be sure you noticed. You noticed?'

'Yeah.'

'He's not so much the boss any more. Maybe some day soon he won't be at all.'

'Who will be? You?'

'It could happen.'

'And it could snow in August,' Jacob said. 'Out of the way, please.'

But Beauty didn't move. 'I got a protector now,' he said. 'He's crazy about me, and he ain't going to let you jack me around the way Sal done.'

'Grant?'

'Crazy, so he can't see straight.'

'Funny, what I hear is he's carrying a torch for his wife.'

'One, she ain't his wife since forever. And two, if he gave a shit about her any more you think that boyfriend of yours would still have knees?'

Jacob felt that Beauty had a point—and, for Neil's sake, was glad to hear it made. On principle, though, he kept relief muted.

'And he don't give a shit about your wife neither,' Beauty said.

Now Jacob did let things show in his face. He did so to give Beauty ample opportunity to consider the advantages of behaviour modification.

Beauty chose to ignore these. 'Richard told me all about that,' he said. 'Business, that's all that was. Make a buddy out of her so she'll keep her mouth shut. Or else he wouldn't touch her with a ten-foot pole. Know why? Her ass is too—'

He'd been watching Jacob's eyes. He knew retaliation would be telegraphed there, and he was right. And had it come from either hand Beauty would have been ready for it. But he was not ready for the heavy shoe that slammed down cruelly on to his bare foot. Screaming with anguish, he was shoved backward over a low-slung table that had supported a modest-sized aquarium. When Beauty fell among the fish Jacob thought for a moment of tramping on his fingers but refrained. Helen had half persuaded him savagery for its own sake was indefensible.

Four pink telephone slips with Cox's name on them were waiting for Jacob on his desk. He also found Herman in his rolled-eyes mode. Pink slips and rolled eyes all conveyed the same message: a posse was forming.

Though Cox's office was mayor-less when Jacob entered, he took no heart from this. He felt the absence as more illusory than substantive. Cox's first words made the point.

'You're going to get us canned,' he said. 'Not just you, both of us. You've been close before, but this time you're going to bring it off.'

Jacob muttered something deprecatory.

In the next few minutes Jacob learned that he was making Judge Grant exceedingly unhappy, and that this harassment of one of Tri-Towns' leading citizens had best cease instantly, or the mayor would know the reason why. 'Commissioner McCracken, too,' Cox added.

'Lickety-split,' Jacob said mildly. 'I mean, that is one fast moving grapevine.'

Cox's all-purpose bullet crashed to the desk, spreading scarification. 'They were in here practically the whole goddam morning. You think that's easy to take? Damn you, Horowitz, do you really believe Judge Duncannon got knocked off by Judge Grant? Not for a damn minute. It's what you do all the time. Rumble and bumble around like a berserk bumblebee, disturbing the peace . . . stinging asses . . . important asses . . . just because you like the way important people say ouch.'

'He screwed her,' Jacob said.

'Who screwed who? What the hell are you talking about?'

'Grant screwed Duncannon.'

'Jesus Christ, Jacob!'

'I'd bet my pension on it.'

'That means you can't prove it, right?'

Before Jacob could answer Mayor Knudsen and Commissioner McCracken reappeared. For the next quarter-hour—a period that seemed infinitely longer—the mayor pontificated, while the commissioner followed like a swished tail, alertly echoing him at tactical junctures. In pink shirt and white Palm Beach suit, the commissioner looked fit and fat in a post-vacation way.

Commissioner Liam McCracken was a man with a single guiding principle. It derived from his political alliance with Mayor Knudsen. He had formed it when young. In his middle years now, the commissioner was far more successful than he had ever imagined he would be. He had a wife he adored, four replicated sons, and a low-key passion for conspicuous consumption. His intelligence was limited but not so limited that he was ever in doubt as to the direction from which manna flowed. In return Mayor Knudsen used and misused him shamelessly, but to the commissioner that was not merely predictable but as it should be.

While the mayor fumed and the commissioner echoed his sentiments, Jacob thought himself into Bedford, Massachussets, where he and Helen and two other couples owned a small fishing shack. It was bright morning there with a freshly stocked trout steam begging to be tapped.

Cox had long since subsided into a sullen, pessimistic silence.

Climactically—it had become his habit—the mayor produced the Tri-Town *Courier*, intending to read aloud that morning's diatribe. He whacked the table with it to get his audience's attention. Pleased with the sharp authoritative sound he had produced, he sought it again but on this downswing caught the handle of Cox's half-full coffee cup, toppling it. Steadily the contents oozed over an array of departmental reports, memos, correspondence and the like. Cox watched the coffee-river crest. Sunk in gloom, he did nothing to dam it. Jacob rescued the cup from the floor, restored it to the desk, and started out. He reached the door.

'Where the hell are you going?—' the mayor.

'. . . going?—' the commissioner.

'To arrest a murderer,' Jacob said.

They stared at him.

Mayor Knudsen turned to Cox. 'Is that true?'

Cox brightened: 'Forty-eight hours.'

'Hell he will, it's a lie,' Knudsen said. 'He lies, and you back him up. Cox and goddam Horowitz, patter and songs.'

' . . songs,' the commissioner said angrily.

'OK,' the mayor said, 'name him.'

Jacob gazed back impassively.

'Damn you,' Knudsen said, 'I've got a right to know. I'm the mayor around here in case you've forgotten, and I not only have the right to know, it's my responsibility to know.'

'Twenty-four hours,' Jacob said.

'Twenty-four—who the hell do you think you are?'

'. . . are?'

Jacob got the door open a few precious inches.

'Horowitz!'

'Sir . . .?'

'In twenty-four hours I'll have that name or your ass. Understand?'

Jacob smiled, negotiated an inch or two more.

'Wait, goddammit!'

He waited.

'It sure as hell better not be Grant,' Knudsen said.

Jacob called FBI headquarters where, over the passive resistance of three intermediaries, he finally reached Slidell. He reported that Grant was indeed connected but that the Family claimed clean hands vis-à-vis Judge Duncannon. He also reported that, according to Sal, the FBI had a porosity problem. Slidell said he knew that, knew who the leak was, and knew, too, that the Family knew he knew.

Jacob's grasp of this was imperfect, but he decided he liked it that way. He was about to hang up when Slidell said, 'What'd Grant want with your wife?'

Jacob took a breath. Then, in a brief, colourful speech he let Slidell know how much the question and its implications offended him.

'Cool it,' Slidell said. 'One of my people was over-eager. Nobody's tailing her any more. Or you. OK?'

'OK,' Jacob said after a moment.

'So answer.'

'He tried to put the make on her.'

Slidell grunted. 'It would be a shame, wouldn't it, if we couldn't bring that switch-hitting son of a bitch down.'

Jacob borrowed a grunt from Slidell's repertoire.

He called Helen. When she answered he said, 'Why don't you ask Amy if she'll tell you where Neil is?'

'Just like that?'

'Why not? What's to lose?'

'She won't tell me.'

'Try.'

'I wouldn't tell me if I were she.'

'Ask her anyway.'

Ten minutes later Helen called back. 'She wouldn't tell me,' she said.

He called Judge Grant and identified him as Judge Duncannon's sexual partner on the night she'd been murdered. There was a silence. Jacob tried to persuade himself it was a nonplussed silence, but he knew better. It was an unflapped, poker-player's silence.

'Will that be tomorrow morning's banner headline?' Grant asked when he was good and ready.

'If so?'

'It would be unfortunate.'

'For you.'

'Yes. For me it would be unfortunate. For you it might be catastrophic.'

He then waited for Jacob to request details. Jacob did not and told himself he had won a small victory.

'*Have* you spoken to reporters?' Grant asked.

'No.'

'Then I take it there's a quid pro quo involved. What is it?'

'Answers to some questions.'

'Ask.'

'To clear the record, did you rape her?'

'No. Next.'

'Are we talking about an ongoing relationship?'

'Once upon a time. Not since her marriage, though. Incidentally, if there had been a rape involved I would have been the victim. Ellie was in a snit that night. Let me rephrase that. She was in an incredibly volatile state—looking for sympathy, out for revenge. Erotically speaking, you have no idea what that combination can . . .' Interrupting himself with a chuckle that became mean as soon as it stopped being prurient. 'At any rate,' he continued, 'I was clearly surrogate for someone or something. You fill in the blanks. For me the point was how much fun emotional instability can lead to.'

'Did you follow her to the theatre?'

'Did I follow her to the theatre and there do her in? I did not.'

'How can we be sure?'

'Why not take my word for it?'

'Your word?'

'Yes, Lieutenant.' Jacob heard the smile. 'The word of an honoured, respected, well-connected, influential community leader. Take the word of a state supreme court designate and, in all probability your soon-to-be governor. Surely, everyone else will.'

Jacob hung up, feeling outmanœuvred.

*

His last call, which he made after staring into space for five hard-thinking minutes, was to Wiley Tait, from whom he extracted directions to his mountain hideaway.

## CHAPTER 11

As it did most fine summer days between noon and two, the tall, slender building caught the sun, transmogrified its rays to liquid, and doused itself liberally—a splashy, dappling effect, the kind of blow to the eye that might have caused a momentary stir even in the Apple. In the Tri-Towns, some miles north, Foley Towers was now in its third full year as the talk of the barbershops, the beauty parlours, as well as a variety of social clubs, backfences, and other similar centres of communication.

No longer referred to as Foley's Folly, the steel-girdered, glass-fronted office structure was today ninety-eight per cent occupied. As a corollary, ninety-eight per cent of the one-hundred-twenty-five thousand who comprised Tri-Towns' population were now backers-to-the-hilt of any such statement as 'Trust Buck Foley to know a good thing when it's going.' The cause and effect implied was no surprise to the hero of this morality tale. While still in diapers Buck Foley had lost a cherished peppermint stick to a blue-eyed little charmer with ribbons in her golden hair and a rock, literally, in her left fist. Never again had he felt real confidence in his fellow person.

Waiting in the hot pink reception room of Foley Investigations, Inc., which filled the twentieth or penthouse floor so vividly, Helen was willing to number herself among those impressed. But as she looked at the pink walls, the pink pile carpet, and the mural-sized portrait of Buck in boots (with favourite Stetson and assorted cowboy accoutrements) pinkly framed, she wondered, not for the first time, where was 'private' in all this? Which is not to say she didn't recall Buck's answer.

'I'm as private as my clients want me to be, pretty gal,' he had said in the Three Aces' back dining-room, the night he tried to recruit her. 'But that ain't it, private. You'd be surprised how few of them give a cow chip about private. What they want is—scalp the bastard. That's why they come to me. They know I'll do it. One or two big ones and suddenly you got the top gun. Plus I sock it to 'em price-wise. They love that. That's the other reason they come to me. They squeal, but they love every centimetre the Bowie knife goes in. Meanwhile I never saw the walk of life showbiz didn't make smoother—which includes, in case you slept through all that, the US presidency.'

The receptionist, a hot pink blonde—barely twenty, extremely pretty, ice cubes for eyes—kept sending measuring glances Helen's way.

Whatever the standards, Helen was sure she wasn't meeting them.

She tried for deeper concentration on the current issue of *Business Week*. As a business person herself, she was hoping soon to like *Business Week*. She hadn't got there yet, however, and through its cover she felt the impact of the receptionist's stare—a proprietary stare, she decided, meant to convey that the blonde belonged in that hot pink ambiance while Helen didn't. That was OK. Helen was prepared, even eager, to agree, but no twenty-year-old chit was going to disconcert her. She lowered the magazine and stared back unflinchingly.

Buck, hitting the reception room with his customary brio, swept her into an embrace. 'Helen, my love, how is every bit of you?'

He held her away, taking the time to inspect the bits for himself.

Experiencing warmth at the tips of her ears, Helen was glad Jacob wasn't around.

But she was glad the receptionist was.

Large, stout, florid, with pinkish-red hair and light blue eyes, Buck Foley had been born in a small north Texas town forty-three years before, a vital statistic he conveyed universally. At the age of four his travelling salesman father had moved the family to Cleveland, where Buck had grown up and gone to school. Far fewer were aware of that.

He hurried her down a long corridor and into the office mainstream, past phalanxes of computer-laden work stations, past the open doors of two handsome conference rooms. Busy, busy people—all in shirtsleeves, all in a hurry, all young. Young Bucks, she thought. Fifty or so chips off the old Buck.

At the edge of Buck's sanctum hot pink met its Waterloo. There the colouration went suddenly protective, sober greys and blues, betokening a proper seriousness now that the troubled were about to get down to brass tacks—the business of making dead certain that particular bastards got specific retribution.

He established her in a beautifully sculpted Eames chair. He then seated himself on the edge of his monumental desk so that he was positioned to look down her blouse if she were careless enough to provide opportunity.

She wasn't.

How's Jacob, he wanted to know when he became convinced of her alertness.

She satisfied his mild curiosity in that direction and then performed her part by asking about Marie and the kids. There were five of them to get through. He did them justice.

After which the phone began its series of interruptions. For the next fifteen minutes or so she watched him operate. She didn't mind that; he was such a virtuoso. She particularly liked what he could do with his voice—basso profundo when he was leaning on someone; light tenor with a touch of vibrato when a female client was in need of the sensitivity light tenors were created to deliver. She enjoyed watching him operate. He enjoyed her watching.

For his star turn he placed a call to Scotland Yard.

When he finished with Inspector Darrowby—a conversation that was mostly, it seemed to Helen, an exchange of verbal leering—he swung towards her, grinning. 'Not bad for a north Texas harp.'

She told him just how much of a hero she thought he was, taking a good long while about it and not tiring him in the least.

'Pretty gal, come work for me,' he said when he was sure she'd run dry.

'No.'

'Yeah, you're right. We'd have a flaming affair, and Jacob would draw down on me before I got my St Paul office open. The one in Minneapolis is already in place. Did you know that?'

'No.'

'That's eight now. All right, at least move into my building.'

'No.'

'I'll make it rent-controlled.'

'No.'

'Why not?'

'We already covered that under Flaming.'

He threw back his head, a big Buck-o laugh, then grabbed and kissed her in comradeship. A hand of his had to be slapped away.

'Pretty gal, what can I do for you?'

She reached into her bag for Ellie Duncannon's memo and gave it to him. He spent a moment with it, but when he raised his glance it was as if he had just read an eye chart. He was now the complete professional—smooth, seamless, ready for the game. She was reminded sharply of just how good a police officer he had been.

'I reckon you're riding out for Jacob on this one,' he said pleasantly.

'Yes.'

He returned the memo to her.

'Buck, don't be like that,' she said.

'Like what?'

'You're acting as if we aren't old friends.'

'Jacob's a friend? I thought he's a cop.'

'A cop who understands about protecting sources,' she said. 'Do I have to tell you that? You've known him longer than I have.'

A doomsday shake of the head. 'Bad business for a PI if the world sees him trackin' 'longside a cop.'

'What's the world got to do with it?'

'The world's the world, pretty gal,' he said with a frown dark as 3.0 a.m. 'We all got to live in it.'

'Jacob says to tell you he'll owe you a favour.'

Up came dawn. 'Well, now, that does change things a bit for this here Buckaroo,' he said. 'Okay, draw one favour's worth and put a head on it. Which means I recognize the handwriting. Yeah, and the style. But if your next question is what do I know about her untimely passing, the answer's not a damn thing. Savvy, partner?'

'The heat's on?'

'Funny about this here coming election. Some think Judge Grant's got it locked. Listen to others, and you get the feeling he ain't got nothing locked, not even his own party's nomination, 'cause lately there's been these skeletons rattling—Big Jake Horowitz being responsible for some of that. Anyways, the thing is on both sides highbinders are goin' on the prod. Me? I just don't cotton to politics in any way, shape, or form. Never have. When the old Buckaroo smells politics he hightails it for the mesa. Gettin' through, pretty gal?'

She dug into her purse and produced a photograph. 'Is this yours?'

He examined it, then returned it. 'There were three Foley hands saddled up for this one, plus a big city freelance. Spare no expense, she said. Talk about wanting a poor bastard scalped. Took us a while, what with the subjects spooked as they were, but I guess we finally got it done.' He took the photograph from her again. 'I sure enough guess we did. Good-looking pair of sinners,' he said, not pruriently but with a professional's quiet satisfaction. He returned the photo. 'Sore as a boil, young Tait was. Tried to bust the company Leica. Got a temper, that hoss.'

'A murderous temper?'

He shrugged. 'Who knows? Not me. Get Jacob to lecture on tempers. His thesis is everybody's temper is murderous . . . even yours, pretty gal . . . given the right set of circumstances.'

'Buck, how long did you have a tail on Tait, before and after Duncannon's death?'

He was on his feet, pulling her to hers. 'One favour just got all used up. Want more from ol' Bucko, tell Jacob to boost the price.'

He walked her to the door of his office where he kissed her cheek, aimed large paws at another set of cheeks, and was foiled only by excellent reflexes.

She had reached the elevator when the sound of high heels echoed behind her: the receptionist, skirts hiked above fetching knees.

'He said this is for you.' Breathlessly. Superb bust all the better for that. And well she knows it, Helen thought. She took the folded piece of paper torn from a five by seven spiral-bound, but before she could read she heard: 'You think I'm a bitch, don't you?'

For the sake of form Helen might have demurred.

'Don't say no, it's true. It's this face. I've got a bitch's face. You're lucky. You have a sweet face.'

She turned to go. Had Helen been able to think of something sensible to say she would have followed her. But she couldn't. The ice-eyed receptionist retraced her steps, the clatter of heels subdued now.

With a sigh for the variegated nature of life as she knew it, Helen examined the paper. She guessed its home had once been a Foley operative's notebook. Suddenly, she had a hunch she might be able to guess its message, too. She unfolded it and learned she was right.

## CHAPTER 12

The Tri-Towns Union League, a mini version of its opposite numbers in New York and Philadelphia, was none the less impressive: two ample red brick storeys, trimmed in white marble. Originally, it had been a showcase mansion. The erratic millionaire, an Irish immigrant turned gold prospector who conceived it, however, went bust once too often, causing him to sell to a group of more stable millionaires. These were Union sympathizers—a number far smaller in the North than school history books about the Civil War lead children to believe. In a sense then, albeit a limited sense, the League's founders had been mavericks. Which was ironic, Jacob thought whenever he was forced to push past its imposing doors, since, from one end of the Tri-Towns to another, no symbol was in its class for stuffiness and hidebound orthodoxy.

He found Judge Grant in the Grant Room, seeming, despite the commonalty of surname, somewhat out of place there—at odds in the same way a piece of modern art might be if surrounded by Greek statuary. It was a large room, filled with Grant photos, portraits, and assorted memorabilia, among them a rusty Grant sword, a torn Grant glove reported to have been recovered at Fort Donelson, several innocuous Grant letters, in one of which the President-General was dunned by a bootmaker for fourteen dollars and thirty-seven cents, and, the prize, several pages discarded from the original manuscript of Grant's autobiography. These, so the legend went, had been discovered by a descendant wrapped around a collection of Mrs Grant's hairpins.

There were two other occupants of the room. Sunk in leather chairs and buried in copies of *Barron's*, they were in their seventies and emphatically dowdy. Old-money dowdy. Brooks Brothers Grant, on the other hand, was a sartorial oasis in the Union League dinginess. He, too, had been buried in *Barron's*, but he lowered it as his glance lighted on Jacob. He watched intently as Jacob crossed the room to him.

'Fish out of water, dear sir,' he said.

Jacob borrowed another of Slidell's grunts.

'In a way I suppose I am, too. The difference between us is that in ten or a dozen years I shall be all but indistinguishable from those old dragons over there. Whereas you . . .'

Jacob smiled sourly.

'What's your verdict, Lieutenant?'

'About what?'

Grant lifted eyes to the ornately framed portrait over the fireplace. It was of the room's namesake as well as his own. 'Am I bogus Grant? Or honest Grant?'

Jacob thought he saw a resemblance and said so.

'Wrong. But don't fret, sir. It's a universal misconception. Guess how it was begun?'

'By you?'

He surveyed the room with exaggerated care—the dragons were still burrowed in *Barron's*—before motioning Jacob to lean forward. 'Actually, it was my great-grandfather Troutman's glove. He never got closer to Fort Donelson, Tennessee, than the Philadelphia armoury. There's a strain of wickedness in me, sir, that is sometimes irrepressible. Have you noticed?'

'Yeah.'

Grant studied him, then sighed. 'No longer friends, I see. What a pity Mrs Horowitz chose not to be discreet. Well, I shall miss our occasional outings. They were a pleasure to me. You were never boring. At any rate I do hope you're not here in the guise of outraged husband.'

'Not today.'

'A shade less Puritanical grimness, if you please. I mean, sir, what is at issue here? Retribution? For what? After a short but therapeutic interval I would have returned the lady refreshed and replenished. And who would have benefited most? Why you, sir, whether you like admitting it or not.'

And suddenly Jacob knew he was in danger of being amused. He had to take a moment to reaffirm his value system. And another to tighten the nuts and bolts of his facial expression. 'I ought to kick you into next week,' he said.

Grant looked at him in distaste. 'I insist we be serious. I wish to know why you tracked me down here. It has nothing to do with Mrs Horowitz, of course. So . . .' He narrowed his eyes. 'Could it be you're a surrogate for the FBI?' He didn't wait for an answer. 'Dusky Mr Slidell is becoming a nuisance, an invasion of my privacy which I'm at the edge of finding intolerable. What shall I do about him, Lieutenant?'

'Get Sal to put out a contract on him?'

'Sal? Contract? Who is Sal? And what is a contract?'

Grant's eyes found his namesake's portrait again, as if seeking there advice on how to deploy his troops. Adjusting the creases of his trousers needlessly, he said, 'I gather Mr Slidell is a determined man, but why, I wonder, is he so determined?'

'Maybe he just can't stand aristocratic-type honkies who go bad. Maybe, in a way, they remind him of plantation owners.'

It was an insight that had started out flip and hopped a

fast plane for serious. Both men were silent contemplating it and its implications. Moreover, Jacob had the feeling they arrived at similar conclusions. It was that until now neither had sufficiently appreciated the extent to which Slidell was a fanatic. Not the kind of fanaticism given to ranting and raving, but the deadlier, infinitely more pragmatic kind; the kind, for instance, that identifies war criminals and runs them to earth thirty years later in a foreign country. At that moment Jacob knew Grant was off his hands and almost, though not quite, felt sorry for him.

'War is hell,' he said mildly.

Grant's tongue flicked at his lips. But at once the mask was back in place. It had serene blue eyes, a smiling mouth, and a basic expression that was a masterpiece of congealed insincerity. 'Be so good as to remind your nigra friend of that,' he said. 'Before it's too late. And now, sir, back to you.'

'I need a fix on your movements between seven and nine on the night Ellie Duncannon was murdered.'

'Didn't we discuss that on the phone?'

'Let's discuss it again, in detail, please.'

Grant was contemplative. 'Curious, the effect you have on me. I see myself allowing you leeway I seldom permit others. Seldom? Never, not since the longed for demise of my father, who terrified me. In my courtroom, sir, people have found themselves up on charges for a tic I took exception to.'

'Yeah,' Jacob said. 'But all that's coming to an end. It's all unravelling now. You know that.'

'Do I?'

'Two weeks, three weeks. Before the election anyway you'll be out of here. Remember where you heard it.'

They stared at each other.

'Seven and nine,' Jacob said.

Grant sighed, took a moment. 'Seven. Dinner hour. Yes, I remember now. I was at my desk. With a sandwich. I despise workaholics and all their ilk, but that night I had no choice. Tremendously busy, you see—' He broke off. And then, dazzlingly, there was the famous grin. 'No, I think I'll tell you the truth. Why not? What a damned amusing thing to do.' He appeared to consider the prospect further. 'Why not indeed? I *was* at my desk with a sandwich from seven to about half past that night, but it had nothing to do with being busy. I was waiting for Ellie to clear people out of her office. I had been trying all day to see her alone. Can you guess why?'

Jacob could. 'Because you'd learned she was wearing an FBI wire.'

'Bravo!'

'Who'd you learn it from?'

Grant waved a finger.

'And when her office cleared?' Jacob asked.

'That was, as I say, about half past seven. I heard a woman hurrying down the hall. I looked out but couldn't see her. When I went into Ellie's office, however, it was empty. I realized she must have been the departing woman. I returned briefly to my own office to collect my briefcase and jacket. At shortly after eight I arrived here.'

'Here?'

'Yes.'

'You're lying, of course.'

'Which time?'

'You're saying now you did *not* make love to Judge Duncannon the night she was murdered?'

'Make love? How Harlequinesque.'

'I could drag your ass down to the precinct right now,' Jacob said.

'Wouldn't that delight Mayor Knudsen.'

Once more their glances locked, but as usual neither yielded much so they disengaged. 'OK,' Jacob said, 'allegedly you arrived here around eight. This place? This room?'

'This very room.'

'How late did you stay?'

'Ten, ten-thirty. Might have been a bit later.'

'Someone can swear to that?'

'Ah, I thoght you'd never ask.' He was silent, savouring the moment. And then . . . with deep, malicious pleasure, provided the name.

Helen, insomniac, was in the kitchen with her pre-dawn potion—warm milk, which she regarded as only a shade less unpleasant than the sleeplessness it was intended to fight.

'Sorry,' she said when Jacob appeared.

Her eyes were lustreless. Her black hair was pulled back Apache-style, so tightly he knew it must be hurting her. It was one of the things she did when she was anxious, as if only physical pain could make other kinds bearable. She looked old. He wanted to take her in his arms, but he didn't. She was impervious just then to comforts of the flesh.

'I hoped you wouldn't wake,' she said. She took a sip of milk and winced involuntarily.

'How can you do that?'

'What?'

'Drink that stuff, detesting it as much as you do.'

'It puts me to sleep.'

'It does like hell.'

Flash of anger. 'I didn't ask you to come down here. Go on back to bed, Jacob. I'll be fine.'

And she did look a little better, he thought. Blood had come up to overwhelm the pallor. She looked alive.

'Damn you, you did that intentionally,' she said.

He smiled.

'I hate being manipulated.'

He went to the cabinet, found the brandy, and poured himself a couple of fingers' worth. He brought the bottle back with him and laced her milk. He tipped his chair against the wall.

Finally she said, 'I think it stinks.' Her glance was fixed

on the table as if it contained a TV prompter. 'I don't think I can cope.'

'So don't.'

Her glance was suspicious. 'What am I talking about? Do you know?'

'Sure. The peeper business.'

She stared at him.

'Pack it in if it bothers you.'

'Just like that?'

He nodded.

Back went her glance. She waited a moment for cues. 'It never occurred to me I'd feel this way about it,' she said. 'I thought if I failed it would be because of all those reasons businesses do fail. No clients. No cash flow. Too much of everything else.'

'And then you got a close-up whiff of Buck Foley's operation.'

'Oh, for God's sake, what do I do, talk in my sleep?'

'Sleaze,' he said. 'Glitzy sleaze.'

He took her cup away and gave her his glass. She sipped gratefully. 'But if I pack it in, Jacob, then what do I do?'

'Something else.'

'What?'

He beckoned to her, so she came around to his side of the table and sat in his lap. 'Do you remember the first time we ever sat like this?' she asked. 'It was in my kitchen. Do you remember what happened?'

'The chair broke.'

Her knuckles struck solid oak. 'I bought this with hulks like us in mind.'

He sniffed at the warm pocket of flesh between her neck and shoulder.

'Jacob . . .?'

'I'm here.'

'I didn't hate it enough, if you want to know the truth. The truth is I could see myself getting used to it. And then maybe I'd actually grow fond of it. Think about that, Jacob. How could you live with someone like that? A female Foley in the house.'

He laughed.

'It's not funny. It's scary.'

Turning her so that she had only him to look at, he said, 'The truth is, it's a job. And it's got a lot of aspects to it, like most jobs. All right, think about it this way. Tomorrow, 3.0 p.m., a person comes into your office and says I lost this child ten years ago. All I can tell you about her is she had this clover-shaped mole behind her left ear. But God, if you could find her. Are you thinking?'

'Yes.'

'So?'

'I should be patient, and it will hapen?'

'You should be patient.'

She shook him hard. 'And it will happen?'

'Make book on it,' he said.

He slung her over a shoulder, not easy, and began the march back to bed, slow and heavy-footed. She protested, warning him against strain, but only half-heartedly. The fact is the effort was pleasing to her—and to him. They delighted in his strength. Not merely because it was equal to the immediate task, but because, in some deep-seated, preternatural way, they construed it as a symbol. They felt safe behind it; outside, wolves howled.

Later she said, 'Jacob . . .'

'What?'

'Who killed Judge Duncannon? Do you know?'

'Probably.'

'You do?'

'Probably who. Probably how. And tomorrow we take a ride into the country and probably find out why.'

'You're a wonder,' she said contentedly.

# EXITS

Now, having come to the wrap-up part of my story, I find it's a lot harder to wrap up than I thought it was going to be. The events themselves are clear enough, God knows, but that's not the problem: it's separating what's germane from what's not. Looking back, I've discovered, is a little like rummaging around in a drawer that's already been rummaged around in. Nothing's where it belongs. Jumbled images. Fragments of dialogue. You sweat over them, dredge them up, only to find, often as not, they have nothing to do with what happened in Wiley's cabin that terrible last day.

Enough. Let the wrapping up begin. Get it in gear, keep pushing, and you figure to wind up somewhere. If somewhere turns out to hurt like hell . . . well, I guess that's what's supposed to happen.

Alec, having missed the point of my bishop move, was a sitting duck for the discovered check that plunged his queen into mortal peril. A moment later he lost it and resigned.

'You're getting real good, Neil.'

He placed a couple of the conquered pieces back on the board so he could study the position that had led to his downfall. Belatedly, he discovered the bishop's duplicity. Then, lifting it, he gently tossed it at me.

'You little bugger, you. Ellie always said one day you'd be good enough to beat me three out of five.'

'She said it to get at you.'

'She could always do that, the bitch.'

But the harsh word was spoken softly enough to take the sting out of it. I couldn't have been his brother and a Duncannon and not known the direction his thoughts were taking: Ellie, how to feel about her. A problem that wouldn't go away, and my problem as much as his. Did we mourn her? Yes. Were we grief-stricken? No. Alive, Ellie was *the* one in the world Alec most loved to hate. But the point is he had expected her to live forever, and death makes revisionists of us all. I mean, I saw things in Alec's eyes sometimes that surprised me, that surprised him even more, I think. We'd been confused about Ellie when she was alive and even more so now after all that had happened. Adding to the complexity—I'm speaking for myself here—was the conviction that it was perfectly possible for her to suddenly appear. Oh, I knew she was dead, all right: (1) cops, lawyers, and reporters wouldn't let me forget it; (2) I had looked into her dead face, seen her dead eyes closed. So what? Reality isn't the only stage on which we exist, and there was a way in which I kept expecting her to stalk in from the kitchen—right then, for instance—to bust my ass about dirty dishes left in the sink. Or for some new failure in ancestor worship. Or . . . name it.

I asked Alec if he felt the same. He didn't answer. He was staring at the chessboard with such intensity I knew he didn't see it, and a moment later he swept the pieces to the floor. He went into the kitchen. Pretty soon he was back with a tray, two glasses full of ice, a bottle of Johnnie Walker Black and some pretzels. By then I had the armies realigned, eyeing each other across the killing field.

He poured drinks. Lifting his glass he said, 'To life. You'll drink to that, won't you, little brother?'

'Sure.' I watched his expression. It didn't contain real enthusiasm for the toast.

'Wiley does himself nicely in his mountain hideaway,' he said. 'Son of a bitch has a lot to thank the Duncannons for.'

The question of gratitude aside, Wiley did do himself nicely. Outside, as rustic a cabin as the one in which A. Lincoln first saw the light of day; inside, it was themed for comfort. Big kitchen; big, booklined living-room; sofas, armchairs, and thick throw rugs all over the place. A fire-place you could walk into. And from all five porchside windows a vista worth a second glance: the lake, small but lovely, particularly showy in the mornings when the sun's rays danced on it. From the back windows, you could see Big Totemac, or Big Toe, Wiley's name for it, the nearby mountain. Of respectable proportions as indigenous mountains went, it stretched tall enough to count on being snow-capped in another month or so. Jutting from it horizontally was Annie's Leap, a long, narrow spit of rock that looked like a modest landing-strip raised a hundred feet or so above the lake. Safe enough for sunbathing and picnicking—even volley ball and badminton playing—it was anything but for diving or leaping. Fifty years earlier a seduced and abandoned servant girl had proved that, according to local folklorists. Did I look at it a bit longer that afternoon than I had on other days? Did I? Probably not. In fact I'm certain I didn't. It's just that now, as I sit here writing this, something in me seems to wish I had.

Alec's glass came down on the table with whisky-sloshing impact. 'Where the hell is he anyway? Wiley, I mean. And Margaret. I hate it when they're both gone at the same time.'

I didn't say anything. I opened a queen's gambit and played both sides for a few sets of moves. I heard him doing this and that, pulling earlobes, rubbing nose and/or chin, but didn't look at him.

'Don't tell them I said that. Either of them, OK?'

I nodded. A moment later I said, 'Wiley drove Karen down to the general store for some frozen pizza and stuff. And Margaret went for a walk right after you conked out on the sofa. About ten winks into your forty.'

'Why didn't you tell me?'

'She asked me not to.'

'Why did she do that?'

Slow-witted Black had just been suckered by White's

craftiness; I made him pay by yielding a knight for a pawn.

'Why, damn it?'

'She didn't want you chasing after her, I guess.'

'Chasing after her?'

'What she said was she had some thinking to do, but you've been watching her like a hawk, Alec. Every tic and twitch. She doesn't like it, nobody would.'

This time he kicked the board. I thought at first it might reach the ceiling. 'Who the fuck's brother are you?'

We stared at each other. I wanted to poke him. I came very close to it, and I think he would have welcomed it. It was a bad moment, considering what Duncannons could get up to, but then I took a deep breath. I managed first to collect myself and next the scattered chess pieces. He helped me.

'Tough times,' he said apologetically.

'Yeah.'

We heard the sound of Wiley's Audi as its tyres left macadam for the pebbled road an eighth of a mile away and came around the bend. I knew it was the Audi, and yet I couldn't help going to the window to make sure. Alec looked at me and I nodded reassuringly. Who else might we have been expecting? Guess.

I watched them debark loaded with packages, Karen giggling at something Wiley had said. This was odd, since all the laugh lines in Wiley's face happened to be non-existent at the moment, but for reasons Karenesque she wanted the world to think otherwise. In skimpy shorts and scoop-necked blouse, my former wife sure caught the eye, but it's amazing, isn't it, how you can know a woman's beautiful and at the same time not care much.

Karen said, 'So quaint. At that store, I mean. I asked Mr Moberly what brand of sardines he stocked. He told me Moberly's didn't go in much for fancy seafood.'

I smiled. Mostly because Alec didn't, and Karen became

irritable when she wasn't appreciated. Wiley had gone back to get something out of the car.

She flitted into the kitchen to put things away. Wiley returned, looking dashing with the arms of a lightweight navy blue sweater knotted about his neck. 'Any decisions arrived at?' he asked.

'Alec thinks I'm ready to throw a scare into G. Kasparov,' I said.

'Who's G. Kasparov?' Then he saw the chessboard and yawned ostentatiously. It was J. W. Black he was interested in. Crossing to it, he poured a drink for himself. He slumped into one of the wicker chairs, long legs stretched to the maximum.

'God, you look cute,' Alec said. 'Just like a movie star.'

Wiley held his glass to his ear, listening to the distinctive timbre of rattling ice cubes. Alec went to the front window and stood there looking out. We could hear Karen clattering about in the kitchen, doing things with cabinet doors—and then talking to someone. Margaret had returned. Even if I hadn't heard her voice I would have known that just from watching Alec's back.

'Wiley,' he said—the tone conversational, one old friend to another. I didn't believe it for a moment, and neither did Wiley. He sat up straighter, braced.

'No regrets, Wiley?' Alec asked, turning to face him. 'Not one damn thing to feel sorry for?'

'You know better than that.'

'Do I? No, I don't. Help me, Wiley. Lay it out for me. Instant replay time. What would you have different?'

'I'd wish her alive. I'd do anything to see her alive again.'

'But the question is, what would you undo?' Before Wiley could answer—not that he was seriously meant to—Alec turned to me and said, 'What do you think, little brother? You're president of his fan club. When he says he's repentant is he a bag of shit?'

Margaret appeared in the doorway. Her face was pale.

'No more of that,' she said tightly. 'I can't bear it, Alec. And you can't either.'

He looked at her bleakly. In a moment she was across the floor to him, her arms around him. He shifted at first as if to fight her off, but you could see he didn't really want to. You could see how much he wanted her right where she was. They clung to each other. And you knew that in seconds she'd start to cry. You thought he might, too.

Wiley left the room.

Karen was in the kitchen doorway, watching. I thought there was more sympathy in her face directed at Alec and Margaret than I had ever seen directed at me. She sensed my attention. Soured by it, I guess, she said, 'All right, that's enough for now.'

They parted, though their hands remained clasped.

'There's business to attend to,' Karen said crisply. 'Or have you forgotten the little matter of why we've convened. Neil, please see if you can get Wiley back.'

I snapped to it. I found him at the lakeside, tossing pebbles and joined in the exercise.

'Your presence is requested at headquarters,' I said after a while.

'The hell it is.'

'Commander Duncannon—'

'Screw Commander Duncannon.'

Face fiery, eyes desolate, he stared at me as if I had something to do with his current state of misery. A beat, and then the excess starch began to ooze from his shoulders. He stooped to gather another collection of pebbles. 'Sorry. I'm not myself today,' he said. 'I'm some other dumb jerk.'

He fired off a small volley. Now a nifty five-bouncer went skipping across the lake's glassy surface. 'I'll let you in on a little secret, old friend. Margaret loves me. She won't look at me. She's kicked me out of her life, but the truth is she can't help loving me any more than I can her. And all the self-sacrifice in the world won't change that. Any other woman . . . Ah, what's the use.'

He found a mini-mountain, scrabbled at it to get it loose, and then heaved it like a shot-putter. I wondered if he was right about Margaret and decided he probably was. And decided also, without much joy, that Alec probably thought so, too. Poor Alec.

'Damn Alec Duncannon,' Wiley said bitterly.

We continued for a few more minutes as this great geological restructuring team and then I said, 'Wiley, let's go. I don't like admitting it, but Karen's right. If we came here to make plans we ought to get cracking.'

I started towards the cabin, but he grabbed my arm. 'Blame him, not me,' he said.

'Blame the man in the moon, but—'

'Christ, Neil, have you heard him on the subject of wooing and winning?'

'Yes.'

He gave me a recap anyway: 'You woo and win a woman, and that's the end of it. After that both parties settle down to their obligations. His is to feed, clothe, and shelter. Hers is to . . . Can you imagine stuff like that in almost the last decade of the twentieth century? Nothing in his chauvinist's creed says he has to talk to her, so he didn't. So she got to feeling *she* had nothing to say. He made her feel stupid. He made everybody else think so, too. It was easy. He presented her as this gorgeous, glitzy collector's item, bought and paid for, wooed and won. Well, who expects more than tits and ass from a collector's item? Neil, he threw her at me. You've never *seen* a woman so starved for attention. I didn't seduce her. Hell, all I had to do was stand still and catch her so she wouldn't fall and break her poor sweet neck.'

'Are you finished?'

'Neil, it wasn't my fault.'

'Sure it was,' I said and shook free.

A moment later I heard him following me.

When we entered the cabin we saw Alec and Margaret sitting close together on one of the sofas. They looked like chastened children. Karen looked like a pissed-off football coach at half time—the team a shortfall to the school, the community, the United States of America, and, most unforgivably, to the coach.

'. . . as its weakest link,' we heard her say, moving into the inspirational part. She liked that so much she restated it for the benefit of the latecomers. 'We're all in this together, a team. A team is only as strong as its weakest link.'

I tried to look like a link of unsuspected substance.

But Wiley, dropping into the chair he had occupied before, said, wearily, 'Maybe it's time to reassess.'

Karen exploded. 'Does that mean quit?'

'No, but—'

'I hate quitters. As you all know, I came into this reluctantly, only because Margaret begged me to. But now that I am in it, I'm in it to stay. It's my thing as much as it's anyone else's. And I won't have anything that's mine diminished by wimpishness.'

He hardly heard her. On the other hand, he would have heard an eyelash fall if it was one of Margaret's. He watched her desperately for a sign. Of what? Of almost anything. Some akcnowledgement that she was aware of his suffering, and that hers matched; that what motivated her now really was self-sacrifice—a gelid, lifeless thing—and not the rekindling of ardour. If he had to he could live with the idea of both of them as victims. He could bear it if they were star-crossed lovers. It was the thought of passion that twisted the knife.

Margaret remained a student of the floor.

It was Alec who spoke. 'If you want to reassess from Buenos Aires, go ahead. I'll buy your ticket.' And yet the tone was less hard-edged than it might have been; curiously, not without a certain overlay of sympathy.

Wiley shut his eyes. When he opened them they were

focused on me. 'Forget I opened my mouth,' he said tonelessly.

I turned to Karen. 'A last-minute word of warning,' I said.

She waited, narrow-eyed.

'It has to do with claiming disproportionate shares of credit. It has to do with slammers, which yours truly can tell you are places to stay the hell out of. And make no mistake—what's being fooled around with here is very definitely punishable by time in the slammer. Unless you think that being a team keeps us somehow from being a conspiracy.'

'Finished?'

'Yes.'

'We've been through all that, Neil, and you know we have. You've had your say about it, and Alec has, too. All warnings were duly issued days ago. We're long past that. Now we're here to nail stories down tight. That's the business before the house and nothing else. Damn you, Neil, you never change. You always want to do it all by yourself, and it's a perfect sign of immaturity, my analyst says.'

'What is? That I'm offering you an out?'

'That you find it so difficult to accept *any* kind of help from me.'

Well, it was a valid enough insight. And the fact is Karen had been remarkably generous—courageous, too—from the outset. And all along I'd reacted with the scepticism that had become a conditioned reflex where she was concerned. Feeling cloddish and graceless, I sought for words to soften the ugly ones. They weren't easy to find, old habits being what they are. In the meantime, however, having flounced to the window, she stood there wrapped in a tried and true martyred silence. Old habits were hard for her to break, too. But there it was, and, watching her, I experienced a predictable lessening of the impulse to redeem myself.

Then suddenly: 'Oh my God!'

Alec and I reached her in a dead heat, in time to see the Horowitz Volvo nosing around the rock garden. Alec turned to me. 'You got the ball,' he said.

'The hell I have.'

He rejoined Margaret. He was grinning, a special Alec Duncannon grin. Conceive of something part derisive, part loving, and rooted in family history. Me in a leadership role, you see, was always enough to tickle Alec, even with hobgoblins lurching around in the wings.

So behold the quarterback, where I guess I'd always known I would be—third and a country mile. With Jacob, like doom, crunching up the path. With nothing in my head except a series of pointless questions, the most thrusting of which was, what were we all doing there? I couldn't have answered that then, of course, though I think I can now. Basic human frailty: fear, shame, self-delusion. In short I hadn't said no when I should have, when I could have easily. Thereafter it was like chasing opportunity on a wooden leg. And what was true for me was true in varying degrees for each of my co-conspirators. I saw that in their faces as I glanced around the room. Oddly, it bucked me up.

'OK,' I said, 'do we make him sweat for it?'

Murmurs. I construed them as universal assent—I didn't dare not to—and moved quickly to build on it.

'Right. Alec, you watch your damn temper. Margaret, choke him if necessary.'

Her response could be described as a smile.

'Wiley, for God's sake straighten up. Let's not be running on our swords just yet. He's tough, but he's not really Sherlock Holmes. And the thing is he's got to do more than know. He's got to prove.'

Experienced actor that he was, Wiley became a warrior king before our eyes, and all I could do was hope it would last the battle.

'Karen . . .'

'Yes, Neil?'

'Be good.'

To my considerable surprise, she hugged me. 'I will, I promise.'

I went down to greet my friends. 'What an unexpected pleasure,' I said.

Jacob looked dour and marched past me. Helen took my arm. She squeezed it, but there was not a lot of joy in her face either.

'Jacob!'

That got him to stop, but when I tried to think of something tactical—or even sensible—to say I couldn't. Still, for some reason, his expression warmed a little.

'Let's get it done, kid,' he said. 'Delay isn't going to help.'

'Where is it written that something has to get done?'

He continued up to the house.

I said to Helen, 'It was all such a crazy accident.'

'He knows that.'

'So why can't he . . .'

'Because he can't,' she said.

'Then the hell with him,' I said and pulled away from her. She caught up to me and got my arm back. And all the way to the house she hung tough, though I wouldn't look at her.

Karen had things stage-managed. Wiley and Alec were at the chessboard, Margaret was doing the Sunday *Times* crossword, and the stage-manager herself was deeply absorbed in Solitaire. For background music she had selected Sinatra with Count Basie. Up-tempo and psychologically bulwarking.

Jacob was appreciative. He even smiled. 'Hello everybody,' he said politely.

*Politesse* to match from those gathered.

Helen asked for a glass of water. I went to the kitchen for it, and when I returned Jacob and Helen were on the sofa occupied recently by Margaret and Wiley. On the coffee table in front of him he had placed a small stack of three-by-five cards. He cleared his throat. 'Your attention, please.'

We responded.

He lifted the top card, read it, placed it on the bottom and then, blandly: 'One of you is a murderer, of course.'

A lone gasp. I'm not sure whose, but it seemed to me female. On the other hand I can't swear it wasn't me. God knows I felt like gasping. Not that Jacob's announcement had come as a surprise to any of us. It was just hearing it out loud in that Sherman tank away.

'Would whoever it is like to confess?'

'I'll speak to that,' I said, raising a parliamentarian's hand. 'And the answer is, where the hell do you get your gall?'

Jacob turned over another of his three-by-fives and said, 'I'll explain myself.'

Alec dislodged a bishop, inadvertently this time. He didn't bother to retrieve it.

'First, let me say that this liars' league of yours, while a pain in the butt starting out has become pretty much okay by me. What I mean is, I understand it. To a degree I even sympathize with it. And I've decided not to use it against you unless you force me to.'

'Liars' league?' Karen said. She turned to me. 'Neil, what on earth's a liars' league? Do you know?'

'No,' I said. And added bravely, 'Neither does he.'

Jacob remained equable. 'A sensible scenario might go like this,' he said. 'The guilty party comes forward. Cuts down on the bullshit. Saves us all time. Earns my gratitude. After that we discuss things constructively.'

But his measuring glances were evenly distributed, no face more honoured than the next. What did that mean? That he truly hadn't settled on a candidate? I wondered if that might actually be so. I doubted it but decided to act as if it were. While I was still sorting all this out, however, Wiley launched himself from his chair.

'Cat and mouse,' he said. 'I hate it. It's disgusting, and I won't put up with it.'

Jacob watched him as if he were auditioning.

'You have a warrant for my arrest, Lieutenant?'

'No.'

'Then I'm gone.'

He made it almost to the porch door before running out of gas. Then he turned. Not to Jacob. To Margaret.

'We don't deserve this,' he said. It was a voice that creaked and quavered and never could have reached beyond the third row, but the anguish in it was compelling. 'What we did, we did. But it wouldn't have happened if—'

Fiercely, she cut him off. 'If we'd been better people,' she said.

That, however, was her watershed. The words out, she immediately bent double as if a fist had been slammed into her stomach. Her hands hid her face. When Alec put his arms around her this failed to comfort and seemed instead to level some final barrier. Choking sobs. She tried to control them, but they ripped out of her, hard, so that clearly the pain was physical, too.

Alec and Wiley looked at each other, hostilities ended. But though the battle was over neither face showed triumph, both showed hopelessness, both looked like death-march faces.

'I hope you're enjoying this,' I said to Jacob.

'Why should I be enjoying it? I don't enjoy stakeouts or electric chairs either.'

Helen said, 'On the other hand, it isn't Jacob who killed anyone, just in case you've gone a little foggy as to why we're here.'

This Helen was not my rallying around Helen, but a Helen with priorities rearranged. And one whose cold-eyed stare could back me off, exploiting as it did the weakness of my position and the strength of hers.

'All right,' Jacob said. 'I guess I better lay it out for you.' Business of consulting cards. 'Let's begin with how Wiley Tait and Margaret Duncannon are lovers.'

Karen said, 'That's a despicable lie.'

Jacob looked at her reflectively. 'The way laying out works,' he said after a moment, 'is I talk, you all listen. Not because I love the sound of my own voice, but because nothing else is efficient. If I ask you a question, you answer; unless I do there's no need to speak. Clear?'

Karen's hand went to her throat in mock terror. 'Oh yes. Oh my goodness, yes. But what if I should *accidentally*—'

'If you do,' Jacob said, 'I'll drag you outside and cuff you to the steering-wheel of my car.'

Karen believed and subsided.

Another card lifted, studied, buried. Whatever else they were the cards were psycho-drama. I knew. I wanted to jam them down Jacob's throat. He saw that. So did Helen, who suddenly reached over mercifully, and took them out of his hand.

'Ellie Duncannon found out about the affair,' Jacob said. 'Sorry, step back one. She began to *suspect* there might be such a thing and hired Buck Foley's crew to make sure. They did. They put the evidence in her hands.' Pause. 'The evidence is . . . irrefutable.'

Some kind of small animal sound, quickly stifled, came out of Margaret. Her face remained hidden in Alec's chest, and he kept patting her shoulder. His own face was impassive. It took me a moment but then I was able to place that particular non-expressiveness. It dated back to the period when with great regularity he was running away and getting caught and being hauled before a variety of authority figures, all eager to foretell his dismal future.

Jacob continued. 'The next day—which was also the day of her death incidentally, or not so incidentally—she confronted Wiley. You lied to me,' Jacob said, confronting him also. 'You told me she cut you off because she was sore at you for being money-hungry. The truth is she was sore at you for being an adulterer. Did you lie to her, too?'

'No. Though I could have.'

Jacob nodded. 'You know, for a while we really did think you were tailor-made for us. Motive, opportunity . . . only thing is, I always kind of liked that half-baked alibi of yours. Just the same I never expected to see it go airtight the way it has. But I guess you don't know about that yet. A Foley agent had you staked out that night. He was up here lurking in some bush and corroborated for you. You ought to be grateful.'

Wiley's gratitude seemed containable.

Jacob turned his attention to the rest of us. 'So whoever killed Judge Duncannon, it wasn't Wiley. Back to Square One. If not Wiley, who else could have inspired Neil here to become a busy beaver liars' league organizer? That's what I asked myself. The answer? Well, you know the answer—Alec, of course.'

He beamed at us. None of us beamed back. Alec retrieved the dislodged bishop and restored it to duty. His hand was steady. But his face had lost colour, while the eyes were glittery and hard to read. Was he getting ready to do something . . . Alec-like? Was Margaret at all alert to the possibility? Oh God, look at her. *Her* eyes were lustreless, her beautiful face blotched and smudged. And so distant. If help were needed it wouldn't be coming from that source. Only enough energy there for despair.

Like tumbril wheels, Jacob's voice rumbled on. 'Hell of a lot to be said for Alec as a hot-shot suspect. His liars' league alibi was blown, and everybody in the Tri-Towns knows he'd been feuding with his sister since infancy. And we also know about his famous temper. Okay, into the slammer with him. Any objections?'

'She'd been raped,' I said, on cue.

'Not rape.'

'Not rape? All right, not rape. Sexual intercourse, carnal

connection, congress . . . whatever. Are you telling us Alec—'

'How disgusting,' Karen said.

Jacob looked at her for a moment as if he were trying to recall in which pocket he'd placed the keys to his handcuffs, but then he said, 'OK, so if it couldn't have been Wiley and it probably wasn't Alec, who then, I wonder?'

We decided to treat the question as rhetorical, knowing he wouldn't. He didn't.

'Not one name comes to mind? Not Richard Grant? I got to tell you that surprises me,' he said. 'Male or female, if it moves it's not safe. Everyone in this room has heard that. You've heard that, Neil, haven't you?'

'Put less crudely.'

'Put it any way you like.'

Where I wanted to put it was somewhere out of sight. Fat chance.

'I'll tell you why that name didn't pop right out for you, Neil. Because it's the bell-ringer, which makes it the last name you'd be likely to volunteer. Let me restate that. The reason you didn't suggest Judge Grant is you knew he did have sex with Ellie.'

'How could I know a thing like that?'

'Because you were in the right place at the right time—that is, just outside your sister's office while it was happening. You witnessed it.'

'How could I have done that? I was with—'

'Amy? Is that a lie you really want to stick to? Because if it is I'll have to bring her in for the kind of session I've let her bypass up to now.'

'Do what you goddam please.'

'You mean that, Neil?'

'No,' I said, and turned away from him.

I went to the window, stared out at the lake, and thought of Amy, glad she wasn't with us; glad I'd held out against Alec who'd wanted her to be. It seemed to me I spent a long time posted there, but when I turned back to Jacob I knew it couldn't have been long at all. In his expression I still saw the same mixture of extremes that had caused me to turn away: pity and pitilessness. No way they can coexist, right? Except in faces like Jacob's.

As if there had been no interruption he said, 'So, after the fact—Ellie's demise, I mean—you conferred with Grant, offering him a chance to stay free of a scandal. Political animal that he is, he jumped at it. Nothing to lose, he told himself. Time enough to come clean—with impunity, mind you—if and when some cop got around to asking the right questions. Yesterday I got around to it, Neil.'

Everyone in the room, maybe everyone in the whole world, was waiting for me to say something brilliant in reply. And I was eager to oblige. All I lacked was the prompter to cue me with the first few words.

Jacob pretended to be helpful. 'Aren't you going to ask me what's the big deal if Grant had sex with Ellie?'

'No.'

'No,' he said. 'Because that was clear to you from day one.' Then, like the snake he is, he turned to Alec. 'And to you.'

The Duncannon brothers looked at each other. I know how tired I felt and how beaten, and my eyes must have reflected this. But what I read in his was something else entirely. Something that scared the daylights out of me. He gave me his patented tuneless hum. And then his patented mirthless smile.

I don't think Jacob liked that smile much either, but after a moment he turned back to me. 'What the hell, let's spell it out. *Grant* had sex with Ellie. Not in the theatre, in her office. It happened . . . say thirty minutes, no more, before her death. What does that mean? It means—as Neil well knows—that we can now separate sex from murder. And *that* means we're no longer forced into thinking of Alec as a pervert, right? Now, if we want to, we can think of him as just a murderer.' Pause stretched to the breaking-point. 'Which he is.'

Alec broke for the door. I'd been half preparing myself for that, and yet my legs were concrete. By the time they were flesh and bone again he had twenty yards on me. He had reached the end of the pebbled path circling the rock garden and had forked left, and I was in no doubt as to his objective.

'Damn you, Alec!'

I screamed it at him, but he didn't even break stride. Linebackers strewn like daisy petals, the legendary fullback had burst into the clear now with the tang of the goal line rich in his nostrils. One chance, and that was to cut him off—the right fork, the sharper climb but the shorter distance. He was the power runner, but I was the rabbit, quicker in a sprint since my early teens. And I think I would have caught him if my ankle hadn't turned just as I reached the first crest marking the beginning of Annie's Leap. I stumbled, didn't quite fall, but lurched about drunkenly for long enough to cost myself half a dozen yards. I was that much short of him when he reached the edge.

'Alec, no! Please!'

He turned. He narrowed his eyes and shook a finger at me. It was as if he had already crossed into that region from which messages come with particular force. 'Margaret,' he said sepulchrally. Half joke, Alec's kind. Still, there was no doubting the underlying seriousness. Either I did a satisfactory job of watching over her, or—if such things turned out to be possible—I should prepare for ghostly visits.

Then, tipping an invisible hat, he stepped off backwards.

I got to the edge in time to see him bounce three times against the side of the cliff before smashing hell out of the water's surface—Cannon Duncannon in life and in death.

Jacob was the first to reach me. I was waiting for him. I swung at his face. I wanted to obliterate it. But he hunched his shoulder, blunting the blow. He wrapped me in a bear hug before I could swing again.

After a while he let loose a little. 'I've seen worse ways to go,' he said. His voice was even, unmoved—an expert's view delivered with professional detachment. It infuriated me.

'It's a stinking way to go. You don't know shit about it.'

'You're wrong.'

I looked at him.

He waited until he felt sure his meaning was clear, and then released me. 'So keep your goddam mouth shut,' he said.

Which is just about word for word what Alec had said to me some weeks back.

# EPILOGUES

## 1

Jacob placed his knight on the square just vacated by one of Helen's pawns and said, 'Check.' It was a crushing check, forking her king and queen.

Helen said, 'I hate this game.'

'You're getting better at it all the time.'

'Am I? Well, you can consider progress at an end because I'm never playing it again.'

She stormed into the kitchen.

When she returned with coffee for both she found him bent over the board, Kasparov's *Fighting Chess* at his side.

'Until tomorrow,' she said apologetically.

'White mates in two,' he said.

She joined him. They tried things and finally saw the Champ snooker Black into accepting a punitive rook sacrifice.

'Kasparov is not a nice person,' Helen said.

'He's a chess player. All chess players are descended from Genghis Khan.'

'That's what Neil always says.' Faintly, delicately emphasizing the name.

He returned to the chess table. She interposed herself, and used her foot to shove the table away.

'Neil?' she said, as if prodding his memory. 'Your neighbour? Your friend? Your very own chess guru? He's about six feet tall with—'

'Enough,' he said.

It was Sunday night. They'd been to dinner at Jacob's parents'. Jacob and his brother had argued politics—mildly, for them—but enough so that siblings were much in her mind. Also, it was a week to the day since they'd come down from the mountain. Jacob-like, she folded her arms across her chest and then stepped back to improve perspective. She thought at last he might be ready to talk. She hoped so because in that instant she had decided he was going to whether he wanted to or not. She'd had enough of Tolstoyan melancholy to last.

'I spoke to Neil this morning,' she said. 'He had his first session with Harry Messenger. He thinks he's going to like him. He thanks you.'

Jacob riffled Kasparov's pages.

'For recommending Harry, that is. I don't think he's ready to thank you for anything else, but he will be.'

'Some say this game was invented in twelfth-century Persia. Others—'

She detached the book from him. 'We both know who you're sore at, and it's not Neil. It's yourself, of course. Damn it, Jacob, look at me.'

'I'm looking.'

'You're not looking. You're pretending to look.'

He grinned, despite himself. 'All right, *now* I'm looking.'

'You act as if you've done something to be ashamed of.'

'Imagine.'

'Oh, for God's sake. You are *not* a person who makes a practice of taking the law in his own hands.'

'That's good, a cop who doesn't regularly take the law in his own hands. Stop the presses.'

'But every now and again—in *everybody's* life—something happens that calls for a special response. All right, suppose the letter of the law had been observed, what purpose would have been served?'

'That wasn't my question to ask.'

'*I'm* asking it.'

'None. OK? It's still a judge's question to ask, not a cop's.'

'How about a friend's? Is it a friend's?'

He sipped some coffee.'

'Alec died to give you a way out.'

His glance was ironic. 'You're sure that's why Alec died?'

Her glance was Apache-distant, the kind he was always uncomfortable with. When he sipped this time he burned his tongue.

'Alec died,' she said, 'for a variety of complex reasons, but his death did give you a way out.' She looked at him. When he said nothing she continued, 'What purpose would have been served if you'd turned your back on it?'

'Maybe I would have felt better.'

She thought about that for a moment. Then, reaching her hands out to him, she drew him to his feet. 'I want you to do something for me,' she said. 'I want you to go down to Anna Shockley's and return the garden shears I borrowed from her. The walk will take five minutes. Mrs Shockley will take another five, gushing and blushing while she tries to hide the horrible crush she has on you that turns her from a dignified middle-aged matron into a simpering adolescent whenever you're in the vicinity—and then five minutes more for the walk back. Fifteen minutes, Jacob. And by the time you return I expect you to have forgiven yourself. I know you, Jacob. I know what gives you the sweats and what doesn't. Being basically wrong does. In this case you were basically right. Take fifteen minutes and get used to it.'

She delivered the shears to him.

## 2

And so, enjoined by both brother and friend, I did keep my goddam mouth shut—for three days.

Three measly days? Not much stick-to-it-iveness evident

there, you say, and I suppose I'd have to concede the point.

Well, maybe not. How about some context? How about seventy-two hours during which I shuttled helplessly between guilt and fury; during which rancour and remorse, heating my bloodstream, threatened thrombosis from minute to minute? How about three days like that? Does that throw a new light on measly? Probably not. Probably you're some kind of Nietzchean superman or philosophical stoic, at the very least.

I had gone MIA.

Helped by Buck Foley and team, Helen found me shivering and whimpering in a gritty little fleabag thirty miles from the Tri-Towns. She dug me out from under whisky bottles, bathed me, shaved me, fed me, brought me home. Then she got Amy to watchdog over me.

At this point enter Jacob's Dr Harry Messenger and his famous breakthrough in therapeutic strategy. Breakthrough: examine your life as a novelist might and generate insights and catharsis in the process. (See *Neurotics, Write your Book*—for six straight weeks last year a regular on the NY *Times* best-seller list; once as high as third.)

'Your life is an interesting story,' Dr Messenger informs patients and disciples. 'Write it that way, and the result will be angst transmogrified into manuscript.'

As any observer of communal behaviour might have guessed, Messenger has not gone uncriticized. One of his colleagues blistered him good recently, opined in a learned journal that if faith-healing rates four on psychotherapy's scale of ten, Messengerism notches two. I have also seen the approach described as mental health, Harlequin romance style. Maybe so, maybe not, I'm no expert. Still, I *can* tell you how hard the technique works against nightmares. Gentles the hell out of those plunging beasts.

At any rate six months of transmogrifying equals a sizeable stack of quality Bond. For quite a while I got a kick out of that, seeing manuscript grow, but I don't much any more. Are there inferences to be drawn? Does it mean the therapy has taken hold? Interesting question. I'll have to put it to the good doctor, who is a nice father figure of a man, incidentally, complete with smelly pipe, shabby tweeds, and six decades of perspective. And who is distinguished from that earlier good doctor in my life, my progenitor, by a seeming awareness of my existence.

OK, so I've been thinking seriously of calling it quits as a transmogrifier. But I guess it wouldn't be cricket (or good therapy) to pack it all in with a major hole unplugged. What's not been revealed yet is how IT happened. Do I hear a rumbling out there, something to suggest a willingness to remain in ignorance? Never you mind. I told you at the outset how limited your options are. IT happened like this.

Millie's: a boutique for trendy underwear. And there, framed by peek-a-boo bras and frolicsome pantyhose, I stood, watching Ellie's building to see who would come out. Grant emerged, took three deep sniffs of night air and set off jauntily down the street. Did I know before that moment it was Grant who had partnered Ellie sexually? Not with certainty, but in a way. You catch a glimpse, an idea forms nebulously, then Grant appears, sniffs, struts, and suddenly I made him, as Jacob might say.

It had crossed my mind to follow him, though for what purpose I'd never be able to tell you, but then Ellie showed up, torpedoing the notion.

Ellie looked nervous. Not merely nervous, strung tight enough to give off twangs from twenty yards away. She looked scary. For a moment I stayed put in Millie's doorway, pretending I was impervious to all this. Brother, I told myself, was not much more than an anthropological term. I could rise above it. I could count up grievances in a blood-thinning way. In short, I tried hard to do the sensible thing which was to head back to Amy and mind my own business. Instead I followed my sister.

Having yielded to tribal instinct, I found myself cutting through the Jessup Street Mall and almost instantly approaching Sunday Square. She had turned once, seen me and said, 'Stay out of this.'

I reminded her I embodied a command performance; added that I would be glad to leave if she came with me; suggested Amy's place for coffee and an opportunity for the two most important women in my life to get to know each other better.

Kabuki masks such as her face had become don't generally respond to conversational gambits. This one was no exception. She saw me clearly in the role of Brother-as-Keeper—never mind how unwillingly—and wanted no part of anything so domesticated. She wanted savagery. Maybe you know how that is. I do. You reach a certain point, and you yearn to kick out. You crave the balm of breakage; the sweet music of shattered glass. Your heart's on fire for the idiotic, and the self-destructive. Anything at all as long as it's violent.

I tagged after her up the stairs, through the empty auditorium, the small one, Second Space, coming to a halt before Wiley's dressing-room. I waited for her to unlock the door and then followed her in, exhaling discreetly on discovering that Wiley wasn't there. Had I known all along it was Wiley she was stalking? You betcha. Any two-year-old and all former husbands would have known that.

She began to pace. From next door the residue of a big laugh told us *Shrew* was going well. I remember thinking, with little relevance and less good sense, that Wiley, having had dark moments about the play during rehearsal, would have been pleased.

'I'm going to kill him,' she said suddenly.

'Ellie, for God's sake.'

'You think I won't?

'Of course you won't. And what the hell are you talking about anyway?'

Kabuki masks are not good smilers either, but she gave it a try. The result was predictably ghastly. 'People in our family do kill one another,' she said.

Whereupon she whipped out the now famous photos.

The shock was substantial. Retrieving them from my nerveless fingers she returned them to her purse, which contained another little shocker—a tiny, shiny little shocker.

'Give me that,' I said, reaching.

She drew the purse away, protecting it behind her back.

'He's a liar and a cheat,' she said. 'We made promises to each other, Neil, of the most sacred—'

The turning doorknob cut her off. She dug into her purse for the tiny, shiny .22 and aimed it with remarkable steadiness. I swung to knock it out of her hand and *missed*. Read that word again, please, because it's pivotal. If my hand hadn't been fisted—if I'd *slapped* at the gun—it seems to me outstretched fingers might have caught just enough of the barrel to . . .

So I shoved her now, *wanting* her to fall and jar the gun loose. She tried to recapture her balance. In the process she managed to get her feet tangled, tripping herself. Even then she would have suffered no more than a bruise or two if she had put a little honest effort into softening the impact. She didn't. She was too intent on keeping that damn gun levelled, as if once off line only God could right it again. Ellie was no athlete. She had her beloved father's angular, awkward body, and it did her in.

Yes, and I collaborated. No one will ever need to remind me of that. The bone-against-metal sound of her head connecting with the sharp, steel-plated base of the desk is still with me. Muted these days, thanks to Dr Messenger, but I know it always will be with me. It bears a fugue-like relationship to another sound—Alec thudding his way down the side of that killing cliff.

Ellie's smile was ludicrously contented, but her skin seemed already to have paled and tightened. A small red pool was evident in the vicinity of her right ear. In one hand she still grasped her friend the revolver; in the other her purse. This had opened, and photos were now strewn all over the room. No pulse. No breath. No heartbeat. I straightened, stared down at her. Another face became superimposed over Ellie's—younger, prettier, my mother's. But the colour of blood seemed identically dark.

I can't tell you how long Alec was in the room before I noticed him. He was looking not at Ellie but at one of the photos, and the sound he made was a kind of keening. I don't think he was conscious of it. He just kept making it. His face was as pale as Ellie's. The moment seemed to go on forever; a time-warp moment. At last it ended. I saw an act of will performed, after which he took a deep breath. He went on his knees at Ellie's side and lifted her hand, though nothing could have been more certain than that he'd find no pulse. He let the hand drop, closed the eyes, rose, and said, 'All right, let's tidy up.'

The only one he could have been speaking to was me, but it was if the language were foreign.

He gathered up the photos and stuffed them in his inside jacket pocket. I watched silently. But when he wrenched the gun free of her grasp and wiped it with his handkerchief, I got some words out in the frog's croak I barely recognized as my voice.

'What are you doing?'

'Taking no chances. No fingerprints at all are safest, I figure.' He tossed the gun to the far corner of the room. 'Let them speculate.'

I started after it.

He grabbed me and threw me against the wall. When I bounced off it, he threw me back again. Then he shook me hard. 'She's dead. Stone cold dead, and you're to keep your goddam mouth shut about why and how.'

'Fuck you,' I said.

This time he belted me—open-handed across the mouth. Only open-handed, but it was enough to buckle my knees.

'You like being a jailbird, little brother? When they send you up this time it won't be for a few months. We're talking years now. We're talking manslaughter maybe. I want you to think about that for a moment. Are you thinking? OK, throw this in. You're no longer just a naughty boy first offender. First offenders get slaps on the wrist, often as not. Hidebound criminals, recidivists—'

'Oh, for God's sake.'

'—who can't stay out of trouble, get time. Hard time. You really want some of that?'

'I pushed her, and she fell. I wanted to get the gun so she wouldn't blow Wiley's head off. I didn't even push her hard.'

'Don't tell me. Tell the Spanish Inquisition.'

I turned away.

His hands on my shoulders, gentler now, turned me back to him. 'She's dead, Neil. Dead, dead, and still dead after all the breast-beating in the whole world. But I know this about her. In her own cockeyed way she loved you, adored you.' He paused. 'Would she want you railroaded for this?'

We set about wiping off surfaces. It was after this he sent me into the bathroom for a last look around. When I returned I saw what he had done to her clothes and came closest then to saying the no I'll always wish I had. He stared me down. He was so certain, you see. So absolutely together and hard in his conviction. And I . . . wasn't. And so he won.

We stood over her for a moment silently. Neither of us had sent the other a signal, we just did it. Saying goodbye, Duncannon fashion.

We left the theatre separately, but before we did I asked him what had brought him there. He told me Ellie had, a call from her. She had something to show him, she said.

Something he'd be very interested in. 'And then she started yelling at me, screaming at the top of her lungs that anyone not man enough to keep his wife at home got exactly what he deserved. In a way I suppose she's right.'

'Alec, she was hurting. She—'

'I knew what she had to show me,' he said, cutting me off.

'You knew?'

He amended that. 'Somehow I guessed.' He looked at me. Then he smiled, eyes hopeless. 'I think I came here to kill her,' he said.

When I was a kid . . . seven, eight thereabouts . . . it's my earliest theatre memory . . . Alec took me to see *Arsenic and Old Lace*. Do you recall the final curtain? The hero, whose dotty sisters have committed that series of benevolent murders, discovers he's not related to them after all. Thus, the woman he's in love with, the future mother of his children, can now relax about heredity. Buoyed by the last-minute revelation, he rushes stage centre and yells, 'Hooray, I'm a bastard.'

The woman I'm in love with has been poring over my manuscript for better than two hours. And I could use a timely genealogical revelation. But, what with the liars' league disbanded, there's not one to be had. For better, for worse I come from whence I come, and I am what I am. You pays your money . . .

She shook her head just now. She's looking up at me . . . she's *crying*. What does that mean?

3

Helen put down her book, removed her glasses, turned off the lamp, and stared into the darkness. Finding no answer there that was satisfactory on all counts, she shoved Jacob and waited out the obligatory protests. When he was sufficiently awake she said, 'I'm up to speed on everything except when you knew it was Neil, not Alec.'

'Not until Alec took off for Annie's Leap.'

'Why right then?'

'Because it was right then I convinced myself it was Alec who started the liars' league. If Alec had killed Ellie it would have been Neil who started it. Neither would have started it to protect himself.'

She thought about that. Then she said, 'Anybody who loves anybody belongs to a liars' league, if that's what you want to call it. I mean you'd lie to protect me. We both know that, though you hate admitting it. And I'd lie myself blue to protect you.'

He pretended to be asleep so he wouldn't have to answer.